T0156667

Call of the Great Spirit / The Fugitive

Gloria Van Rooyen

ISBN: 978-1-4669-9528-4 (sc)
ISBN: 978-1-4669-9527-7 (e)

Trafford rev. 05/21/2013

 www.trafford.com

North America & international
toll-free: 1 888 232 4444 (USA & Canada)
phone: 250 383 6864 ♦ fax: 812 355 4082

Dedication

This book is dedicated to my husband Anthony, Son Burton, Daughter-in-law Lynette, Grandchildren Greer, and Lloyd, Sister Rosalie, and Sisters-in-law Augusta, and June, and my very dear friend Lyn.

My sincere and grateful thanks to you all for having confidence in my abilities and for your encouragement.

**VENI VEDI VECI,—SOLI DEO GLORIA =
I CAME I SAW AND I CONCOURED,
—ONLY GLORY TO GOD.**

Acknowledgement

My sincere and grateful thanks to Anita Howse for teaching me to become computer literate. Patience is her virtue and her grace. I will always love you Anita.

Also to my dear friend and mentor through whom I have attained all my diplomas over many years of arduous study, Professor Denise Leathem and Shammah Ministry.

Contents

Call of the Great Spirit

The Fugitive

Call of the Great Spirit

Chapter 1

The beings had been told that there is trouble in their country, and that they would be summoned to a great gathering of the clans. The usual method of using mist signals would be sent from one clan area to the next, telling them all when the "INSTRUCTION MEETING" was to take place. Every adjutant placed his observers at the watch posts, and anxiously awaited the news of the signal. When the alert came they would all go and join in the ceremonies, at which their clan "HEALER BEING," would go into the sagacity lodge with all the others to cleanse their spirits, in order to welcome the Great Spirit, from whom all wisdom comes.

The clans that would assemble were the NAMARA, CARTY, MAURE, DONALD, KAY, CULLAN, NAUGHTON, NAB, and the CLOUD. After five moons had gone the mist signals were being sent from the first watch post and on to the next until the supreme ruler had been informed.

Each adjutant took his healer being and a few warlords with him, and they all headed to the "CLOUD HILLS" where they were instructed to go. The governing parties all had many miles to travel and it took much time to forge rivers, mountains, and valleys. My name is Maeve and many moons ago when my ancestral grandmother-being told me that we came from a long line of "FEMALE HEALERS" I thought that it was just a story that she had made up. On her death bed she made me promise that I would do all I could to reinstate the "FEMALES" into their rightful place within the clans.

From the ages past these gifts were handed down from the grandmother, to her daughter and so on until there was an uprising, and the adjutant had an "INSTRUCTION MEETING" and decided to excommunicate all the females that had been appointed into this position, until there were no more females trained in this service. The males were strong and powerful and ruled in all areas, and their females were treated like rejects. The horse-beings and the dog-beings had a much higher status, and were treated with much more respect. Every time the wind whistled through the trees, I could hear her voice and the echo sounded loud and clear and I knew that an unusual event was about to happen.,

She was the screaming "benside spirit", crying out for justice to be done. All the dreams I had were of her beckoning me to follow her on through the lands of the 'Dragonfae" not only did I dream of her calling me, but she shook me until I woke up. Then I realised that this was no dream, this was real: she had materialized.

---

*   Lucy Cavendish- Lost Lands

Now she spoke to me and said, "IT IS TIME FOR YOU TO GO AND DO AS I ASKED!

FOLLOW ME I WILL SHOW YOU A SHORT CUT, DO NOT FEAR I WILL BE THERE WITH YOU COME NOW WE MUST MAKE HASTE!!."

I took a few things with me to wear and something to eat, and got approval from grandmother being who was weaving her way through the trees, at great speed. I shouted out to her "Please slow down for me to catch up with you, I am still hybrid-being and we can not go as fast as the spirit can!" she shouted back to me

"WATHAMERA CAN'T WAIT CHILD HURRY AS FAST AS YOU CAN; WE MUST SERVE TO PLEASE HIM. HE KNOW'S HOW TO AVENGE." I tried to keep up with her but had to ask her to let me rest for a little while. When we got to the river she let me rest, now I know how the horse-being feels, and my love for this animal increased. I was not allowed to bring my horse-being because they sometimes snorted, then everything was alerted, and your hiding place was revealed. This was very serious if you were hunting for food or tracking some thing. I had to go on foot, and be very quiet, even quieter than the mouse and the vole. I sat against the tree trunk, and drew the energy, from it into my body and my spirit. I needed every bit that I could get, as I had to swim the raging river. Many times even the strongest swimmers were pulled down, and never came up again.

This is what happened to our mother's people, they were very strong swimmers, but the churning of the waters and the hidden rocks, were a danger that even they could not avoid. The shrill voice of my ancestor, brought me out of day dreaming "Come now the Great Spirit "WATHAMERA" gets restless we must make haste.

Near the tree that I was sitting under was a large log, and I knew that they float. I pushed and pulled but it just would not budge. Then my ancestor screeched out, "ROLL IT TO THE RIVER BANK GIRL." WOW why did I not think of that, I questioned myself? With super hybrid-being strength that I knew could only be help from the spirit gods and the ancestors; I managed to get the log to the swirling waters of the river. I clung to it for all I was worth; it was taken at a terrific speed. Banging into every submerged rock and tree stump in the flow to the sea, wherever that was. I had no idea as I had never seen it, but some of the adjutants had, and they said that all the rivers flow to the sea. Well I was hoping that I would not go into it, because they said that it has no end just like the sky. "Oh! Wathamera I do not want to spend the rest of my life on this log in the water, please make it stop, I begged." After much time had passed the river was not so strong anymore, and there was a bend where the waters parted. One side went to the mountains and the other side I think must go to the sea. I paddled the log towards the mountains and at last it came to rest against the bank. I jumped off and then heard the wailing of my "ben-side" ancestor. She was pointing to the Cloud hills and said, "THERE GIRL, GO THERE, HURRY BEFORE THE CLANS GET THERE TO RECONCILE AND BEFORE THE DEBATES BEGIN."

Chapter 2

When I got there no one was there yet, only the lodge of sagacity stood between the rocks that loomed up on all sides of it. This lodge was very well protected from the winds and the rain, and also very well hidden from the sight of the passers by. Only the "HEALING MALES," knew where it stood. I crept between the rocks at the back of the lodge and hid there waiting for all the parties to arrive. The Cloud Hills were in South Dragonfae', and N.E. of Wythetha. The clan living closest are the CLOUD who came from Dakthea. So were the first to arrive and pick a camping site. They are famous for war, little wonder their adjutant was named, Poison Arrow, and their healing being was known as Foxglove. The NAMARA, CARTY, and the MAURA, lived in the ASTON district. I was very excited and kept a constant lookout to see who would arrive first, and also where they would set up their bivouac clan shelters. I assumed that they would be in

5

close proximity as they spoke the same language, it was the Ahapascant dialect.

I was not at all surprised when the NAB and his healing-being Kinenaught and their warlords were the first to arrive. They were followed by the DONALDS, adjutant Begupriz and Esprayah, then came the KAY clan and riding behind them in mixed company, were the CULLAN, and the NAUGHTON.

The warlords all camped behind their respective adjutant and healing-being. The large rock was in the centre of the space that was surrounded by all the bivouac clan shelters. Now it was time to select the main speaker for the "INSTRUCTION MEETING." It is customary for all the adjutants to choose a tree and mark it in one spot with a circle of poison ivy. Then the archers took turns to shoot an arrow at the mark and the one closest to it, or preferably in the middle of it was the winner and would do the honours. I held my breath, as I knew that this was the one that I would have to deal with. The time would come when I would have to make it known that all the quean and the female spirits in the valley of mirth, wanted the old method of quean medicine female-being's reintroduced. Also that I had been elected to accomplish this by the end of the meeting. I started to shiver at the thought of this very difficult task that had been allocated to me. Then I felt someone shake me and I thought that my hiding place had been discovered. I turned slowly, and was relieved to see the smiling face of my grandmother-being's spirit, she whispered you will do well my beautiful and wise grand-daughter, do not forget that. I am with you, and so are all the spirits of the ancestors that had been outcast from their calling.

Immediately I felt as if the weight of the Cloud Hills had been lifted from my shoulders, and I breathed a sigh that almost shook the chosen tree. The time had come for the archers to take aim, and they were all very close to the mark but it was the Maure adjutant that got his arrow right in the centre of it. He was not as fierce and brutal as the others, and his healing-being WISE OWL never got his name for nothing. He was known to listen to all the conflicts of his clan before he made a decision. Now Mitzion the spirit Goddess of the queans would be happy and I am sure that my ancestors were doing a dance of great expectations, that all their suffering would be avenged.

Chapter 3

The Maure took his place in front of the chosen tree, and gave the signal for the drums to beat out the command for silence. This having been accomplished he called for the plaintiffs and the informers to come forward and make known what the problem is in the land so that all present could hear.

This would then be discussed by the assembly and when a solution was found all the adjutants would sit around the great rock of restitution and a decision would be made. Maeve knew that the problems would not be solved so quickly. In fact she was so sure that they would have to resort to the HEALING-BEINGS going into the lodge of sagacity to get advice from the ancestral spirits, and maybe the GREAT SPIRIT himself would have to be consulted.

The complaint was voiced by all the warlords; they said that discontent had spread throughout the land because the initiates had decided that, the rules to become warlords were no longer acceptable to them. The age limit had to be adjusted because there were many initiates that were strong and accurate enough with the bow and arrow to become warlords, long before the stipulated age. They stated that unless they could do the warlord test by the age of eighteen years, all the initiates from all the clans that were contesting this policy, would assemble and prove their point with an unexpected attack on the warlords of each clan.

They then told them that it would be the adjutants of all the clans that would be abducted first, and be held in a previously selected and secluded place, until the warlords either surrendered, or their demands were met by the agreement of the supreme ruler. Shock and disbelief echoed throughout the Cloud Hills as each member gave vent to their feelings of anger, at the arrogance of the initiates. The fact that they even questioned the ancient laws of the past, never mind that they still threatened to have them changed by acts of war on their own people, was more than enough to resort to all the HEALING-BEINGS having to contact the spirit world for a solution. This would have to be done as the situation facing the clans was critical. A few warlords were told to make a fire in the lodge of sagacity, and also to bring a container with water to which certain herbs had been added by the hermit sage, that would create steam and enhance the trance state. These instructions were immediately carried out so that the steam would soon fill the lodge, and they would all be enlightened by the wisdom of the Great Spirit.

Then the Maure asked if there were any more questions to be answered. This was my cue and I crept out of my hiding place and revealed myself by stepping into the circle. Now a loud exclamation of surprise went up, and I was chided by all for attending a meeting of this description, and told to leave immediately, as this meeting was for male-beings only.

They threatened to make me an outcast and send me to the valley of the lone wanderer, where I would have to live the life of a hermit until the Ghost rider came to snatch my spirit. I replied and told them that I have been sent by the spirits of my ancestors to make a claim to reinstate the queans as official HEALING-BEINGS, as they had been for all the ages past. The males were warlords and hunters and the females were gatherers and healers and communicators with the spirit realms. I had been instructed by the spirit of my grandmother, and told to announce that the decision for this reversal was a direct command from the Spirit Goddess BLITHE. The males would not accept what I had said, and demanded that I should enter the lodge of sagacity with the male healers and see if a female was strong enough and wise enough to stay in the lodge for the required time of the cleansing. They all burst out laughing and pointed at me, daring me to take up the challenge. This I did knowing that I had all the power of the spirit queans behind me, and that the great power of the spirit of Blithe who had sanctioned this to be done would be leading me and teaching me how to overcome the conflict that was bound to ensue. I went boldly forward and took my place last in the line of those who were going in to receive wisdom from the GREAT SPIRIT WATHAMERA, but what they were not aware of, was that I too was going to receive wisdom but from THE GODDESS SPIRIT BLITHE. I was aware that this war was not going to take place neither in THE CLOUD HILLS nor in the valleys. This war was going to take place in the realms of the spirit world.

At the Zenith of the universe is a cosmic Orbis of revolving concentrically arranged celestial bodies that produce a harmony by their regular movement. It is at this pinnacle that Wathemera, Blithe, and Mitzion have their abode. The intermediaries mysteriously speak the Devine words of wisdom to the ben side and the angelic realm. They were all created by the Ancient of times in the Ordovician era about five hundred million years ago. Through the atoms and nebulae there was an evolution of ungodly aggressive shape-shifting creatures, they lived in the labyrinthine underworld of the sphere known as Idiomia. They envied those created with Devine wisdom and they vowed to outwit them with their own evil sagacity. Their means of communication was telepathic, Wathamera's was prognostication and Blithe and Mitzion communicated via the frequency modulation of audiology. And so the credence of virtue and malevolence had its genesis. An endless war was to take place in the firmament, an ongoing battle of shape-shifting wit and Devine Wisdom.

Chapter 4

We all took our places around the fire, that was now so hot that the males started to sweat and so did I.

A long time passed then the chanting began, the MAURA started slowly and the others joined in, and it built up into a high and low tone of A . . . AAH . . . HAA . A . . this was the repeated sound to the beat of a solitary drum outside. I was so amused that I never gave it a thought to chant. I was just watching with great interest, when suddenly someone yanked my ears, and the voice of my old grandmother's spirit whispered

"CHANT WITH THEM YOU FOOLISH GIRL, I CAN SEE THAT I HAVE LOTS TO TEACH YOU, GET ON WITH IT NOW! A . . . AAH . . . HAA . A . ." She began and kept on prodding me in the ribs until I did as I was told. I started to chant with the others and was feeling so hot that I silently asked BLITHE to help me if she wanted me to stay until the end as I felt like fainting, I could no longer get my breath. Instantly there was a cooling breeze on me and BLITHE spoke to me her self. "I am sending the cool air to you my child it will help, no other will get this blessing from me, and you will be able to stay as long as it takes. Now remember that you will soon enter the supernatural realms, and the answers to the problems of the community will be given to you alone. This will be the proof that the intermediaries between the living beings and spirit status must be returned to the queans guided by the GODDESS MITZION. You are now undergoing trance inducing techniques that will incite visionary ecstasy, and you will go on the spiritual quest for the deep and hidden secrets that are known only to the GREAT CREATOR SPIRIT WATHAMERA.

We are all here to support you and when you are victorious a sign will be given that no one can deny."

As we kept the chant to the beat of the drum, I felt an altered state of consciousness taking over, and then the voices of many spirits joined together in a melodious song of welcome. I was told that I had inherited the powers, so now I have been called to complete the plan that the Great Spirit had for my life. I was the reincarnation of COR the brightest star in the constellation of URSA THE BEAR. Not all queans (unmarried healer woman) inherit the powers from the ancestors. There are some who have a calling on their lives, and have to go through the lengthy training required. On completion of this training they are never as powerful as those who have inherited them and the ones who have reincarnated with inherited powers are even more capable of "ethno hermeneutics" as well as all the other fields of the lore. As I became more aware of my surroundings, I saw the spirits of the medicine males that had gone on to the valley of mirth, since the old custom had been obliterated. They were all standing on the right side of WATHAMEARA; BLITHE was next to him and all the spirits of the previous healer females were standing on the left side of BLITHE. Thor the god of thunder was very infuriated that this conflict was going to take place in the firmament, and he gave vent to a loud rumble that echoed right down in to the valleys, and the mountains shook from the impact of the reverberation.

Although Thor was voicing his disapproval of what he thought to be egotistical drama, the thunderclouds issued huge drops of rain that plummeted earthwards, the entranced humans in the lodge of sagacity were totally unaware of the elements. They sat like immortalized beings awaiting the announcement of their claim to fame.

The huge drops turned into balls of ice which had the density of rock that had petrified over billions of eons. When these ice balls repeatedly smote the large rock formations of the CLOUD HILLS deep cracks appeared, and in many places the parts that broke away came falling down on to the lower regions. The adjutants and the initiates trembled in their bivouac, but not one of them gave any indication of being afraid. They knew that the GREAT SPIRIT was angry, and began the chant that would bring clemency. The storm was developing with more fury than any of them had ever experienced. The chanting became more intense and the volume reached the highest pitch that could be attained by the vocal cords of the beings. But Thor had no mercy for the ones who had defied the custom of their nations, with regard to the spiritual duties of the queans. The louder those in the bivouacs chanted the more it angered Thor, and the ice balls got larger and came down with tremendous impact on everything below.

The rocks came down in larger and larger chunks and the Adjutants and the initiates heard them crash against other rocks and trees, splitting them into fragments of what they had been. They were expecting to be crushed under the weight of those that fell, so they kept on pleading for the storm to stop, but it went on through the day and the night with ever increasing ferocity. What would the following day herald? only time would tell!

Chapter 5

Although the ice balls and the huge drops of rain had abated, the storm still raged with gale force winds.

No one dared to go outside for fear of being taken by the north wind, this restless wind that never ceased for days on end. This was an ill omen and one that put the fear of the GREAT SPIRIT'S RATH into the heart of all the beings. The lodge of sagacity had been pounded by some dislodged rocks, and inside the only thing that moved was Massasauga the rattle snake hybrid that had sought refuge from the storm. Eventually the storm died down and the adjutants and initiates ventured out of the bivouacs. Not one of them had been hurt and they took an oath to discuss the changes that had been demanded by the initiates and the queans. They went to the Lodge of sagacity to see if there were any solutions from the Healer Males that had gone to consult in the realm of the spirit world. When they approached they were amazed to see that the lodge was almost flat on the ground, and went cautiously then they heard the rattle and hiss of the snake. The adjutants lifted most of the rocks and when they took the top of the lodge off they were horrified at what they saw. All the medicine males were dead and Maeve was still sitting in a trance with the snake coiled around her. It seemed to be protecting her from any danger, but the males, insisted that the rattler be killed so that they would be able to check if she was still alive. However this was not to be as it uncoiled and slithered out of what was left of the lodge. Almost instantly Maeve opened her eyes and stood up then glanced around her and saw the chaos and destruction that had taken place during her time in trance. She also saw that all the males around her were dead, and the shocked look of disbelief on the faces of the people gathered around made her get the shivers.

They stood in silence and just stared at her, and then the air was filled with the sound of a thousand wailing bensides. The night was dark but the moon was full and they all witnessed the spirit riders in the sky as they past in its luminance. As they went by the distinct sound of the owl hooting was enough to convince them all that their healer male WISE OWL who was now in the wonderful spirit realm, was telling them that MAVE was to take his place, and the other chosen queans to take the place of the ones that joined him in the spirit world. This INSTRUCTION MEETING was terminated after all the adjutants agreed that the queans must be reinstated into that honourable position and the MUG OF MEDE was passed around. However there was still the matter of the initiates to be considered, and it was mutually decided that this matter would be solved at a future gathering. The new order of the quean HEALER FEMALES would be in consultation with the GREAT SPIRITS in order to obtain the answer to the initiates demand. Now it was time to get on the horses that had been spared in the storm, and go home to their respective clan areas. They mounted their horses that were looking in the direction of the rock face and there in plain sight were three distinct carvings of the recognizable faces of much loved females who had ruled as healer females, and since crossed over to the spirit realm. COR, IRIS AND VIELIA, this was the sign that the GREAT SPIRIT GODDESS BLITHE said that no one could deny. The entire assembly stared at this wonder creation in absolute amazement, and they were all speechless.

When they arrived in their own clan village with MAVE riding in front, all the queans and married females knew that she was victorious and a cheer went up followed by the victory dance of the quean ancestors. Maeve knew that she had much work to do and the next day she started on her quest to replace and name all the new quean healer females. She had been told by BLITHE that from now on she had to be known as COR as she was her reincarnation. Her name meant THE BRIGHTEST STAR and that the replacements would be called Sharminn from this day forth. BLITHE told COR that she would give all the new names to the queans herself and that the new order of allegiance would be carved in the stone wall of the clan assembly forum.

Chapter 6

COR told the adjutants that she wanted all the
SHARMINN to come to the assembly forum
for training purposes. The following week they
arrived and all was agog in the village. All the SHARMINN
gathered around the stone bust that was carved in the likeness
of the first Cor to receive their instructions. COR sat in front
of it and did the chant of the necromancer, to raise the spirits
and bodies of the dead quean SHARMINN. All those who
had served in this position with her, came in answer to her
call. There was a westward wind blowing and with it came
the echo of many horses galloping. Then there appeared from
out of the dust cloud all those that had been killed. They were
riding astride the NIGHT-MARES that had belonged to
them in a previous lifetime. COR ordered that they should
stand behind the ones that had now taken the honourable
positions, in the clan to which they had belonged. They all

obeyed and then she introduced the living to the spirit of the entity behind her.

These recalled spirits were instructed to teach their replacements in all the scopes related to their calling. Now they could all go home happily reunited with their ancestor helper entities, and take charge of the healing and spiritual requirements of their clan beings.

COR could see for miles around as the village was situated on a very high hill, the dales below looked very dry and there was hardly any grass for the Cattle and the Deer, that is why they are absent now she said to her self. I must have a rain dance here so that THOR the god of Thunder will hear my cry to the skies for the rain gods to send water from the upper world. She thought that she would go and meditate at the "SHARMINN'S TREE" as it belongs to all the realms, the roots to the under world, the trunk belongs to the middle world that is inhabited by the hybrid-beings and hybrid animals and everything that lives and grows there, and the top belongs to the upper world where the sky is and the spirit world is. As COR was the co-creator with the ancient of times, and was now reincarnated she alone was able to perform all the functions of a SHARMINN. The others only had certain specialalities; this is the reason that COR has to do regular visits to all the clans. The apparent phenomena can be explained by the soul concept. When the lost soul of an ill person is retrieved and purified the illness of the individual is cured. This is also the case when a female is infertile the SHARMINN can obtain the soul of the hoped for child and infertility is reversed. Every living thing can be helped and cured when the infectious spirit is banished by the SHARMINN.

After having meditated for most of the day at the tree, Cor felt exhilarated and was ready to gather the SHARMINN in her camp to perform the rain dance. That night the fire was lit in the village square, and Cor led her clan to form a circle around them. Then she started the rain chant all the natural sounds via onomatopoeia, ascended into the universe taking with them the hope from the hearts of the people. The beating of the drum allowed them to achieve an altered state of consciousness thereby forming a rainbow-bridge between the physical and the spirit world. The acoustics have a neuro-physiological effect that makes them believe that they are ascending into the upper world. COR was now able to exchange information from her world with the upper spirit world that she had accessed through this mystic and symbolic traditional practise. While in this state of ecstasy she was shown the great PHOENIX BIRD rising from the ashes, assuring her that her chosen SHARMINN'S SPIRITS were already active and performing wonders in their clans. He also confirmed that the colours she had chosen for her SHARMINNIC BIRDS were perfect, and that because BIRDS are seen as messenger spirits their feathers would be noticed by all. BLITHE told her that each clan was only allowed to wear the colour feathers of its own clan SHARMINN. This was to introduce a uniform effect that would distinguish them from each other at a distance.

COR agreed to convey the order that had been bestowed upon them to each clan individually and in person.

Now she pleaded for rain to fall on the dry earth so that all the grass and trees would be green and then all the cattle, wild ox, and deer and the wild fowl and duck would return to the hills and dales. This would bring the blessing back to the people, as they would have everything they needed to live a healthy and joyful life. The spirit world reverberated and consent was given for the rain to fall on the parched earth. The people were slowly brought back to their normal state of mind by the rain falling on them from the thunderclouds above. COR received her honour as a very powerful SHARMINN and they all got to dance in the rain celebrating the victory.

Chapter 7

Due to the reincarnation of COR from the ancient of times she possessed stronger power and capabilities like omnificence. She could access information that went decades into the future and also move faster than anything created, she also retained the memories of events long forgotten by any living thing. COR could remember when there was only darkness and also when the light first appeared. She remembered when the GREAT SPIRIT had commanded the waters to gather, and when the land first appeared. She also remembered that it was then that she was sent to the mountains along with her band of SHARMINN to await the coming of all life on this planet Hybrid-beings, animals, trees, grass plains, grains and herbs and the development of all these things and other things that evolved from this first creation. The phyto-geographical and linguistic considerations were made by the SHARMINN. The seeds of all the trees and grass and all the plant species were given to them and they were told to scatter them there. The winds would come and distribute them all over the earth and they would take root and grow when the rains fell on them. At that time all the land was one large piece of ground with mountains and rivers, and a very great extent was just ice. Over ageless time the seawaters separated the land at various points and so the continents came into being. THE GREAT SPIRIT made hybrid man and put them on the earth and told them to multiply and also all the animal species. Then COR decided to stop her dreamtime and get back to the present problem that she still faced. The rebellion of the initiates, and the ultimatum given to the adjutants. That was before the queans were reinstated as SHARMINN.

COR requested that all the adjutants and initiates attended an instruction meeting to be held once again in the Cloud Hills.

On the day that they arrived she asked the adjutants to sit in a ring around the GREAT ROCK and have a very large mug of Mede. The initates were instructed to stand in long lines behind their own clan leader and wait for the answer to their question. COR went to meditate beneath the carved out faces on the mountain, then she came down and performed the ceremony of the early religious incantation worship with swaying movement in accolade to the Great Spirit. During this event the spirit spoke in a loud voice and told the initiates that the age limit would stand firm as it always has been. Should any initiate question the command of the GREAT SPIRIT in this regard or any other they would be struck down by a disease that was incurable by the SHARMINN, and would not go to the valley of peace, mirth and joy. Instead they would be banished into the realm of the evil spirits, and have to endure eternal punishment. When the GREAT SPIRIT HAD SPOKEN the earth shook and a wide and deep abyss appeared. Far below there was a mass of red hot liquid bubbling and swirling from which the most foul stench was being emitted. The initiates were convinced and vowed not to rebel or retaliate in any way.

The solution having been given and accepted, the young ones were sent to hunt for fowl and rabbit to eat at the evening meal. They brought back plenty to cook and eat, when all their hunger was sated, COR announced that all people of every clan were to wear an amulet around their neck for protection from evil and harm. She instructed the young ones to be in charge of this very important errand. They were to find coloured stones and when they had enough, they must bring them to her for purification and to be impelled with the powers required.

The following morning when the first rays of the sun appeared above the mountain, they set off to find the coloured stones. There were some pretty shining alluvial stones in one particular area and they collected as many as they could. In the area of the river there were stones that had no colour but they shone and sparkled in the light of the sun, so they collected lots of them too. Then they discovered some pieces of rock like stones that had a yellow shine but they were not translucent, where as the other colours were all transparent. These were quite large and were found in lump formations, so they took lots of these to COR. She was very happy to see them returning that night, having been announced by the wise old owl.

In the morning she looked at the stones and saw they were very special indeed, undoubtedly sent by the spirit gods and the ancestors. She told the young ones to sort them into piles of the same colours and when they were ready they must tell her. COR then purified them by placing them into containers filled with water to which she had added herbs and the salt from the earth. These containers had to be placed in direct sunlight for the duration of the day after which they had to remain exposed to the moonlight until it declined. Then they were taken out of the containers and left to dry in the sun. Then COR told them to take all the stones that were the same colour as their SHARMINN'S feather colour to her their healer and tell her that these amulets were sent by the GREAT SPIRIT and all the people had to wear them for protection.

Chapter 8

When they arrived in the village lead by COR and all the initiates behind them vocalizing the chant of atonement, a victory cry went up from all the people. They were welcomed by all and sat down to a luscious meal of spit-roasted deer, wild fowl and wild crushed grain that grew near the river. Then it was announced that the GREAT SPIRIT had given a command that all the people were to wear an amulet for protection. COR then explained that each person was to wear this amulet in a small pouch around their neck. Each amulet had to be the colour of the SHARMINN of the clan's feather. However the MAURE clan had no colour as COR means the brightest star, so she choose the sparkling stone that shone and twinkled like a star. All the females were told to make the amulet holders out of strips of hide and hang them around everyone's neck. The MAURE were to wear all the colours of the rainbow in feathers as all the colours of the rainbow could be seen in the stone from the GREAT SPIRIT, and this was their right because the reincarnated COR as SHARMINN belonged to their clan. The young ones went to look for all the coloured feathers that they could find, and every day they found some. Black and white, blue and yellow, red and green, purple and pink, brown and grey, then they sorted all the colours into piles that were the same, and the people had to pass one at a time and collect one of each colour to make the rainbow celebration bonnets.

One day there was a large cloud of dust on the far horizon, and the initiates on watch alerted the clans.

Then the thundering noise was heard and everyone shouted with glee "THE WILD OX ARE COMING". Yes they were headed their way, and it was time to hunt. They needed the meat to dry for the winter months and also the hides for clothes, and boots and night blankets. More houses had to be built as the clan was growing. Each year more babies were born and the extended families had to enlarge their living areas. All the hunters mounted their horses, and then COR gave her permission for the young ones to join in the hunt. The whoop of delight could be heard for miles, as they echoed through the mountain crevasses and all the surrounding hills and valleys. The hunting party stood on the slope of the hill just beneath their village and waited for the lead hunter to signal the charge, each one had his spear at the ready. The dust cloud got thicker and the sound of hundreds of hoof's resonated in the air and all around the mountains. Every one was excited at the thought of killing a wild ox and receiving the honour of being the supplier of all they needed.

Many of the hunters were hoping to impress the lady that they thought was the most beautiful and also gain her affection. The stampeding herd rounded the bend and came into view, and the lead hunter told the youngsters that this was their first hunting lesson. He explained that if they went now they would most likely be trampled to death, so they must wait until the huge animals had all gone past. Then they must follow them, and as they got tired of running they would slow down, and start grazing on the sweet new green grass.

He said that then was the time to go down slowly and aim at the nearest ones. He told them that they must be quiet otherwise they would frighten the herd and they would take off again. They all listened attentively and saw that the wild ox running in the front were starting to slow down when they saw all the new grass. Then those behind automatically ran slower until the whole herd had stopped, and started grazing. Now is the right time for us to go said the leader, who was the most experienced of them all. "We must go over there and then start to creep up on them as the wind is blowing from the wrong direction here, they will smell danger and we won't be able to get any." Now he led them over to the far side of the small hill and into a gully where they could hide and take aim at the ones closest to them.

They were instructed by the leader to kill only four as it would take the rest of the day to skin them and cut the meat into thin slices for drying purposes. The women took the hides and started to clean all the flesh off of them, and then scrape them until they were smooth and spotlessly clean. Then they made a hole at each corner so that they could thread a string of previously dried hide strips through the holes and hang them up in the trees to dry. The strips of meat were first rubbed with salt and dipped into a preserving potion that COR had made from an ageless concoction, that was passed down from generation to generation. After this process all the pieces were hung on drying racks that the hunters had made according to specifications that had also been passed on from father to son since the very first hunt. Now it was a very dangerous time as the wolves and other carnivorous animals could smell the blood and the fresh meat. COR instructed some of the young ones to accompany the hunters on a night and day shift and that they would be relieved by replacements every few hours. This was to make sure that no animal came into the camp unnoticed to steal the meat and hides.

Chapter 9

For the inexperienced initiates there was the feeling of pride, as well as quite a mixture of emotions between excitement and fear. Naturally none of them would admit it but challenged each other to a contest of rivalry, each striving to gain the honour of warlord capability and status.

There was a chill in the air and the clouds were hiding the moonlight. Every now and then you could hear the owls hoot from near and far and the howl of the wolves advancing in their direction.

They were eerie sounds and the young ones started to panic but hid it very well, not only from each other but from the warlords as well. Suddenly there was a vicious growling and snarling coming from the right. They all had their spears ready to strike at the animals heart area, hoping to penetrate it when it lurched it's self at the chosen target. If only the moon would come out from behind the clouds so that they could see them when they approached, now they just had to rely on instinct and say a prayer to Wathemera for protection. The first wolf jumped onto a well experienced hunter and he stabbed it right in the heart without hesitation. The animal fell to the ground and never moved again. One down but how many to go? Instantly there were so many attacking that they thought the whole pack had come down on them. Each man stood his ground and fought back with such ferocity, stabbing again and again until the wolf either went limp and dropped to the ground or yelped and fled in the direction from which it had come, leaving a blood trail for the trackers to take up in the morning. The leader warlord told them to gather the carcases and put them in a heap so that the women could skin them, as the hides would come in very handy for the winter.

They all started to drag the carcases into the place indicated by the leader warlord, then someone let out a blood curdling yell. He had just grabbed a human foot and all the others went to see what had happened. Then the warlord examined the body and announced that the young man was dead.

He immediately sent another man to sound the alarm by making a clanging sound striking two rocks together, at the assembly forum. It was only a matter of minutes and all the villagers came in answer to the alarm. Cor inspected the body and confirmed that the youngster was indeed dead.

His parents were inconsolable, and his mother kept on shouting no, no, Wathemera why did you take our son from us? He was only eighteen years old, no, no, why? why? The woman all tried to comfort her and Cor made her a mug of warm mead and another concoction that would help calm her and enable her to sleep.

The father said that he would make a coffin hewn out of one of the trees that his son always used to sit under when the days were too hot, and his friends offered to help him. All the females made a burial robe from the softened skins of young deer. The parents decided that he would be interred near the peak of Ben Novite, as that was where she gave birth to him just eighteen years ago.

The day arrived and his fellow night watchers carried his coffin up the steep slope, and all the villagers stood around the grave. As the coffin was lowered into the ground they all sang the traditional hymns that were used especially for these occasions. After that an engraved stone was placed at the head and a small evergreen shrub in the middle. This would forever mark the grave of a very brave young male that gave his life in the line of duty.

Life in the small village went on from day to day, hunting and gathering and preparing for the winter that was fast approaching. All the high areas had a covering of the first snowfall and that indicated that it would not be long before the big freeze set in. The men had almost completed the extra layers of thatch grass covering over the roofs and piled rocks and large stones all around the outer walls of their homes. This they did every winter so that there would be more insulation to ward off the ice cold weather, and sometimes the sheets of ice that formed on them. All this hard work was well worth it, and helped keep the warmth from the hearth in the house during the very long and very icy cold winter.

Daily they had to feed the few hybrid cows that they kept for their milk, and also the hybrid horses that did the transporting of their hunted and slain deer, and also all the harvested grain and whatever the woman had managed to gather. It was usually nuts, seeds, and wild berries, also neaps and corn and whatever fruits that they could find. These animals were sheltered in a cave near the village houses and were safe and warm.

However on one extra cold night the evil shape-shifting mohound creatures from the sphere of Idiomia, decided to leave their underworld labyrinthine to go and test the powers of Cor. They loosened all the animals in the cave from their tethers, and chased them into the icy yonder.

They then shape-shifted into the animals that had been in there and kept fooling the men that came to feed and milk the cows, brush the horses and clean the stables. This went on for a few days and the people of the village started to become very ill one after the other. As it was so cold no female nor children went outside, so they never realized that there were other sick people in the village.

The males that took turns to go to the cave started to talk about the sickness in their homes, when they met at the stalls to clean. It was through this that they realized that many people were ill and decided to go to Cor and tell her about the condition. Immediately she realized that the evil ones had infiltrated the village and guessed that they were shape-shifters, going to bring tragic death and kill all the villagers. So she told them that she would make a potion that would cure the illness and all would be restored back to health again.

She said that she would then go and address the situation in the cave. While Cor was busy attending to all those that had fallen ill with the dreaded pox-en the males returned from the stables running, panting and yelling URSINES! URSINES!

Chapter 10

Now Cor knew just what they had in mind, she knew that this was to test her powers, and she was going to go all out to prove to them that the female spirits of Blithe and Mitzion were her constant companions and that nothing could be hidden from her. She had a great secret that none of them would ever guess. She was COR the brightest star in the constellation of URSA MAJOR, the great Bear, and as such URSA is her animal power spirit and so she never had to shape-shift to become a great bear. Ursa was her protector and came immediately when she sent him her distress alarm.

He was also empowered with the magic necessary to change anything into whatever he wished to.

Now when Cor sent the alarm she did so by holding both arms stretched out up to the universe, with fingers splayed and loudly intoned the chant of materialization, while lasers of lightning, emitted from each finger calling her spirit animal to come to her aid and sanction vindication for the entire village.

Immediately the great bear came in answer to her call, bringing other members from his home star with him in order to assess the situation. Cor embraced them all and thanked them for coming, then they went into the assembly forum to discuss the situation. Cor explained everything to Ursa and his companions. Ursa laughed heartily in his deep growl like voice and said to Cor "My dear child you are so new in this position that has been bestowed upon you, and are not used to taking command of unusual situations yet. You know that you are Cor and can work any magic trick that you wish to, you have been given powerful abilities my dear, just be confident and speak things into materializing. Dose our very presence here not prove this to you? Just remember how powerful you are and act on your intuition it won't let you down. Remember that Blithe and Mitzion are always your shadow companions and wise councillors. You will soon get used to it and I will always come when you call, but this problem you can fix yourself. Now run along and turn some of them into mice and the others into malkins. Farewell and best of luck." And in a flash they returned into the cosmos.

Cor was thunderstruck and could have kicked herself for being so foolish, and not thinking further than potions and cures for all ailments. She had a learned good lesson and she remembered it for the rest of her life down here on earth. NOW WATCH OUT she was on the path of vindication and went directly to the cave and did just as Ursa had advised. The mice ran for all that they were worth but the malkins caught them and ate them. "Well said Cor I do not know much about the digestion of a malkin, but you are now going to be here as malkins of solid rock and no rock can shape-shift after my curse has been cast on you. You will stand near the entrance to the cave as rock malkins and be ever aware that you are entombed, with no way out. You will be observers of everything that comes and goes but will be unable to partake in any event. You now have the same fate as the Great Sphinx of the Egyptian desert. He is the spirit of a cursed being entombed just as you are. He will be forever under the constellation of Leo with his Lion shape that is what inspired me to turn you into malkins, and have cat shapes.

However there is a huge difference because you are under my own power sign of Ursa Major the Great bear, and there is no sign more powerful than that.

One can say that their destiny was carved in stone, and whenever the children of the clan caught a mouse they held it by the tail dangling it in front of them singing "MALKIN come and get it, here KITTY, KITTY! The entombed shape-shifters must have been irate but had to suffer as they knew that there was no escape now or ever. The evil shape-shifter Mohound Gods of Idiomia were powerless against Cor and knew that they would have to think up new strategies of evil sagacity to out wit her obvious Devine wisdom and power.

Chapter 11

At last the ice and snow started to melt and the climate improved gradually to the warmer one leading them into the spring. This was the most exciting season of all as there were new baby sprouts of every living plant food starting to show their heads above the very last of the light snow covering, that could be seen every here and there. The wild animals were also giving birth to their young and it was so joyous to watch the antics that the new babies got up to. Sometimes it seemed that they were putting on a star performance just for our pleasure. All the clans held a thanks giving ceremony for the gifts that Wathemera blessed them with each year. After the ceremony there was a meal second to none with lots of mead and much merriment. The dancing and singing went on from dawn to dawn and needless to say everyone collapsed from utter exhaustion and had more to eat and drink than was necessary, consequently they slept for many hours mostly due to the overindulgence of mead that induced the obvious euphoria.

Cor was the only one that kept watch over her intoxicated clan, being the supreme leader she never partook in more than a dram of mead at any one time and therefore was capable of performing her duties. While her clan slept peacefully she decided to do her sharminniac meditation and gain more wisdom from her spirit councillors Blithe and Mitzion. So she started the chant for spiritual transmutation and instantly they appeared before her. "You are doing very well Cor brightest shining star in the constellation of Ursa Major, in fact you are now being called the diamond star, the name correlates with your amulet dear one, what is it that we can advise you on?" "Oh! Thank you for coming to me, I am very uneasy and I feel that there is going to be havoc very near to our village, I fear that Ben Blaver is about to spew hell fire and brimstone and I desperately need your wise council" "Yes you are correct in your thinking, the God Vulcan has been convinced to bring this tragedy upon this area by the Mohound God of the shape-shifters of Idiomia. They could not win over you with your powers and protection of Ursa the Great, so now they have reverted to another tactic, hoping to spring a disastrous unexpected event upon you. You must go and wake the clan and leave everything behind as there is little time before this event will take place, the blessings of Wathemera are with you all go now!"

Cor went and woke all her people collected the animals into one heard and they left at lightning speed, down across the trossachs, and up and over the cheviots until Cor felt peaceful once more,

Then she stopped running and told the clan to rest on this brae.

They had hardly sat down when they felt the ground tremble, and a deep and frightening rumble started in the direction from which they had just fled. Then a deafening blast followed and they could all see the fire and brimstone shooting high into the atmosphere, and a flowing river of magma issued from the vent at the apex of Ben Blaver. This river flowed at a tremendous speed and a substantial volume of molten magma flowed in the direction of the sea. All this red hot magma took everything in its path with it, sparing nothing at all. The clan sat stricken by the realization of their own mortality. Slowly they consciously returned to the reality of what they had just witnessed, and mayhem took over causing them to react with various states of chaos characteristic of their individuality. Cor stood up and raised her hands skywards each finger issuing the laser lightning, this act brought their attention to her and she calmed them all down. Now that they saw their supreme leader calm and in control the panic left them and there was not a murmur amongst them all. Cor told them about her feelings and the apperiation of both Blithe and Mitzion her spiritual councillors and about the advice they gave her. Once again Devine wisdom won over evil sagacity.

She told them that she would conjure temporary bields as shelters and that they would be a nomadic clan until they found a suitable place in which to construct a new village. She said that her powerful protector Ursa the great bear would select a safe haven for this purpose.

Chapter 12

They were happy wanderers gathering everything that they found that would be useful in the future.

Although there were districts that they went through that were so parched that nothing grew there and there was also no water to drink. It was at times like this that made Cor feel like Andromeda the chained lady in the northern constellations of the universe. Cor went on her knees and begged Blithe and Mitzion to help her find water, but their reply saddened her immensely. She was informed that Wathemera the Great Spirit creator had decided to let them suffer for a while as they showed little appreciation when there was an abundance of everything. He said that he would send relief before there were any fatalities, and that Cor must explain why they were being punished.

They felt ashamed and vowed that they would repent and be thankful for everything they were given from Wathemera.

Then they all lay face down and sang the hymns of restitution for their gratitude of the abundance from Wathemera. However the time had not yet arrived to send the relief that he had promised, and they struggled on in the blazing heat, with someone fainting occasionally.

This went on for another day and then Wathemera exonerated them, and fulfilled his promise to Cor.

There were swishing sounds coming from the cosmos, and then they saw her in all her majesty coming down to save them from dehydration and certain death. Aquarius the water bearer bringing the promised relief. Cor magically produced vats in which Aquarius poured the water for them to store. She also produced mugs for each person to fill from the vats and drink until they had quenched their thirst. Then they all lay prostrate and gave thanks to the Almighty Wathemera.

Now they had a plentiful supply of water but no food. Cor told them not to worry as she knew that the delightful smell of fresh water would bring any animal and bird that happened to be in a nearby vicinity, rushing in their direction, and the hunters could bring them down with their arrows or spears. Not long after that the first few birds appeared in the sky, and the hunters took aim and their arrows hit the mark and down came one bird after another. The females started to clean them and prepared them for spit roasting. Thankfully they had gathered some dry sticks during their wandering and Cor worked her magic and started a fire over which they could roast the birds.

The only animals that they managed to heard with them when they fled were two pregnant cows and some horses. The clan were prepared to die rather that to eat any of these as they were vital to their future survival. Soon the cows would give birth and then they would have milk again and hopefully the calves would be one female and one male.

The clan remained there for a while to get some strength back and to rest their weary bodies, as there were some very old beings and also children that would not be able to keep up with the stronger and younger adults. Everyone lay prostrate once again to give thanks and praise to Wathemera the great-spirit. Cor decided to name this the brae of forgiveness, as she names every thing and place as they wander around, according to her perception of it. When the first rays of the sun heralded the dawn, Cor decided to climb the brae to the summit. From there they had the most spectacular view of the countryside that seemed to go on forever. Beautiful big trees and shrubs and luscious grasslands, and the best of all a wide and winding river of the most pure sparkling water, was seen by all. There was a simultaneous exclamation of utter surprise, and then thanks and praise to the Great Spirit Wathamera.

They all ran down the Brae of Forgiveness ready to explore the wonder that was a very unexpected gift from Wathemera. They had only looked ahead but now turning a bend to the right of the brae they saw the never ending sea. Oh! Wonder of Wonders there was more than they had ever hoped for. Surely Cor would choose this paradise as their new home, and yes!!! She did just that.

The clan were delighted and requested that they celebrate with just one mug of mead each.

Chapter 13

Because of the drought and the cursed poxen many clans started to migrate from their homeland.

Some meeting each other as they wandered aimlessly, and made friends. Others were lone clans that had not met any other self like beings at all. They just went on until they arrived at the large river that went into the sea. Eventually they all ran into the various migrating clans and they became one large crowd of people searching for the supreme leader and a paradise to settle in and build a village. By the time they reached Cor and the Maura clan they had been settled in their village for two years and were well established. When the other weary and disheartened clans arrived Cor went to meet them and welcomed them with a feast of deer, fowl, grain dishes mixed with fresh fruit and berries.

Naturally there were barrels of mead brewed and aged for a few months. They were all so pleased to have finally landed in paradise, and the big bonus was to find the Supreme leader right there too.

On the following day Cor told them that they were no longer lone clans but a united nation that she had named the Caledonians. Now they would just keep their clan name but she had put a prefix to it. They were all MAC, and so the MAC clan was a very extended clan, for example The Nab were now Mac Nab, and the Carty were now the Mac Carty, Kay were Mac Kay, and so on. Cor's people were now all Mac Maura. She was quite pleased with herself and at the very first gathering of the clans in the assembly forum Blithe and Mitzion appeared in the middle of the forum for all to see.

They congratulated Cor for the wisdom that she had used in joining them all together; they told her that they would be a mighty nation of warlords that would be unbeatable in combat. They warned the Mac's that they would soon be attacked by a savage tribe that would come from the world of permanent ice. Also that they would not be able to communicate with them as they used signs and grunts when communicating with each other. These beings were a hybrid of partly homo sapiens and another species known only to the Ancient of times, and were known in the spirit realms as the scourge of the great spirit that named them the Hittilas.

The Mac clan had built their village in a large glade surrounded by a forest of coniferous trees, and it faced east. This place was very beautiful and the view from the brae that it was built on included the large river entering the sea. The beach sand was snow white and here and there one could find the shells of the large crustaceans that had died and washed up on to the beach. While playing with one a boy blew into a hole at one end, and was so startled by the sound that resonated through the forest that he let it drop and ran home, to tell his father about the frightening noise that it made. His father Hamish Mac Tavish went back with the boy to investigate this strange noise as he had also heard it but never knew what it was. This shell was conical in shape but with a pointed projection where the orifice was. Mac Tavish realised that what his son had found had great potential, he blew into it with long and short intervals, then it struck him that this could be used as an instrument to summon the clans to assembly, or used as a device for warning, depending on the specific tones used. The sound could be heard from a great distance and Cor went in the direction of the sound.

There she encountered Mac Tavish and his son sitting in the forest and it was them that were making these echoing sounds. They showed the shell to Cor and gave her a demonstration of how it worked, and suggested that she consider using it to summons or warn the clan. She was delighted and accepted it and their suggestion. She decided to call it the horn of plenty uses. All the males that did the day and night watches had to practice the different signals to alert the clans of a particular event.

The females wove the thatch grass into elongated baskets held at each end by men that dragged it through the water at the inlet. They caught many different species of fish, and also the various crustacean delicacies that were abundantly available. The Mac clans were healthy and happy and got tremendously strong from the nutritious food fresh water and clean fresh air. There were always sounds of laughter and music coming from their village.

On a very misty day there was a sudden alarm signal from the watch tower, and it continued repeatedly, warning of danger coming from the direction of the forest. All the females and children were told to go into their homes and stay there no matter what! The Mac clan males were armed and ready to fight who ever or what ever was coming their way. They stood silently waiting in anticipation of just what was out there. There was much grunting and growling among the trees and then a sudden rush of what could only be the beings that Blithe and Mitzion had warned them about. They were large and hairy and walked upright, grunting and growling, their skulls were not shaped like the clan hybrid beings but were broad and flat and so were their noses and ears. They rushed ferociously at the Mac's wielding wooden clubs, and the Mac's faced them head on with their spears and bow and arrows. Two Mac's went down seriously injured but not dead, and seventeen, whatever's went down but stone dead? Then they retreated into the forest and the injured Mac's were taken to the healer females to have their wounds attended to.

Chapter 14

Cor and the Mac's went to examine the bodies of the slain beings and Cor said I must give them a name. She decided to name them Moloch as she was almost sure that they were a second cousin to the Mohounds of Idiomia. The Mac's had made rafts from the branches of the forest trees and bound them together with the dried strips of the deer hide, these they used to float on the sea in order to spear the large fish that never came near the shore or the inlet. Cor ordered the fisher men to load these creatures onto the rafts two at a time and row out to the coral atoll on the horizon and dump them out there for the huge fish to feed on. Now while Cor examined them she got inspiration from Blithe and Mitzion to work her magic and shape shift the whole Mac clan into identical looking beings the next time they decided to attack the Mac's. That would confuse them as there would be females and children and males that all looked like them, walking around in the village guarded by Cor's protector spirit Ursa. That would mean that they would not know if they were attacking their own families or not. But the Mac clan would know the difference and they could wipe the whole tribe out, into extinction. Yes! That is what she will do, the Mac clan would get rid of the scourge of the Great Spirit "Hittila", the Moloch would be dealt with once and for all.

Meanwhile on the sphere of Idiomia the shape-shifting Mohounds were contriving a plan of their own. Deep in the labyrinthine underworld they gathered for a meeting to discuss a new strategy of attack on the Mac clan. The Mohound leader had not forgiven Cor for cursing some of their kind and turning them into stone malkins for the duration of eternity. Now he was calling on all the evil sagacity from their long departed ancestors. They started an intonation of screeching and screaming and diving in and out of the cess-pools to cover themselves with the foulest stench that was so unimaginable, that nothing living and breathing could live after inhaling this putrid odour. They were convinced that they would entrap the entire population of the Mac village by surrounding it after the midnight hour and they would all die in their sleep. They needed allies and thought that the Moloch tribe would be just the right ones to initiate into their own den of iniquity. The evil Mohound leader went and approached the savage Moloch tribal leader. He first shape-shifted into one of them so that he could communicate with them and have no misunderstanding at all. He promised that if they conquered the Mac clan he the Mohound leader would hand over the entire Mac village to them. That would mean that they could settle in a well established village and never have to roam around aimlessly ever again. The Moloch tribe all agreed and they set a time for a meeting to arrange the best way to address the situation. They were so excited that when the Mohound leader eventually left after observing them for quite sometime, they all climbed into the trees and went swinging from branch to branch letting vent to their emotions, with loud grunts and squeals.

Up and down they all went making such a noise that all the owls started hooting a warning, as they had never heard such a commotion before. Cor heard the owls' warning as the echo of it was very well amplified by the surrounding mountains and also the forest. She signalled the watch-tower to blow the alert call on the horn of plenty uses. This would summon the entire Mac clan to assemble in the forum immediately. Within minutes they were all there and Cor told them that something was very wrong in the forest, and that they had better all be on guard in case the Mohounds were preparing another surprise attack but with a different strategy.

Sure enough there was an attack but not from the Mohounds, it was the Moloch tribe that foolishly believed the mohound leader, that he would give the village to them if they conquered the Mac clan. The entire tribe of Molochs came running out of the forest wielding those silly wooden clubs and screeching at a volume that no hybrid vocals had ever reached. They were easy targets and the Mac's arrows never missed anything that they aimed at. One by one the Molochs fell to the ground but those at the rear turned tail and headed for the safety of the forest. Then the Mohounds made their move and shape-shifted into great eagles, and flew down in spiral dives attacking from above.

When Cor saw what they were going to do she gave everyone present a demonstration of her wisdom and power. She manifested a huge transparent ledge that covered the entire village, and one by one the mohound eagle-hybrids hit the ledge at a speed that broke their necks, and they fell down. Cor was just about to give a signal to take them by raft and dump them in the Atoll area to be devoured by the large predator fish that lived there. Suddenly three carline witches appeared, they had long crooked noses with warts on, huge staring eyes that reflected a dark red colour their chins almost touched their noses; their teeth were larger than the horses teeth and here and there was a missing one. They were dressed in black and their nails were long and twisted, and they all cackled in a harsh cacophony of discordant tones. This was enough to upset anybody's equilibrium, but Cor remained in control and politely inquired as to the reason for their visit. We are here to assist all your victims and return them to health and to their beloved home the den of iniquity, the cess-pool of all evil sagacity. Do not think that this is over Cor, we will return to do battle with you at a time secretly chosen by the supreme leader of the devil Mohounds. "Beware O' mighty Cor, your time-honoured reign will end!" Then dark red rays of laser light shot out of their eyes and in an instant there was not a mohound, Moloch, or carline witch to be seen anywhere.

Chapter 15

The horn of plenty uses sounded, cautioning the arrival of an unknown and not yet encountered enemy approaching from the left. Cor went to investigate, and from a vantage point saw that they were indeed a strange looking type of homo-sapiens, they were all blastie dwarfs. They were merrily following the thane chief leader of their species, singing hoo, hoo, hoo, hee, hee, hee, a wee clay jug of mead have we. Cor never moved but was so fascinated by the blasties and all the actions that they were performing while on the move, that she just watched them and almost gave herself away but managed to stifle a few laughs just in time. Some were chasing each other and the one caught would receive a good amount of tickling from all those chasing him. Others were doing cart-wheels, and yet others were doing leap frog, some were singing and others were tripping whom so ever was in their own little dream world, and not aware of all the little tricksters and their various pranks.

Some of them started to chase the ground squirrels, and the mice, others were after the spiders, and ants, the butterflies, and dragonflies, were also not excluded. When they all sat down to eat and have a good measure of mead to wet the whistle, Cor decided that it was a good time to introduce her-self and make their acquaintance.

"Hello there!" She called out waving her arm in the air," and the top of the morning to you all" they got so frightened by the loud voice and the big woman that made it that they all huddled together and screamed GARGANTUA, GARGANTUA, and the entire band of blasties passed out.

Cor was so upset that she had frightened them to such a degree that they fainted. She worked a little magic cantrip and they all recovered. They were still a little bit dazed and just sat staring at her absolutely dumfounded. "I am so sorry that I startled you, I just wanted to say hello and tell you that you are most welcome here," Oh, thanks be to the great spirit they all shouted, we thought that you were going to swallow us all in one gulp" "I am Cor the supreme leader thane of the newly formed nation of gathered previously lone clans. Where do you come from, and what are you called?" "We are the SMA and we hail from nowhere, we are a caird clan that just wander along and sleep where we find ourselves to be at the setting of the sun. Then we make our bield shelter from the tall thick grass or under great rock ledges. It sure is a good life that the Great Spirit has given us."

"Now tell us Cor where is your boundary mear so that we do not enter it in ignorance." "You are very welcome in our village, and you can stay as long as you wish and then be off again if that is what you want to do." "Thank you very much may we stay with you this night and we'll be on our merry way as soon as the sun peeps over the Ben" So they followed Cor to home. When they got there they all held hands and formed a chain, the leader hanging on to Cor's hand. Needless to say she was bent over double and then again in order for the SMA to reach and hold on with a tight grip.

Cor signalled for a meeting and the watch blew on the horn of plenty uses, for the clans to gather at the forum. When the ear shattering sound blasted and echoed from all directions the entire SMA clan fainted once again. Cor just realised that if the sound of her voice was frightening then the blast from the horn of plenty uses must have almost killed them, after all their ears were very delicate, and she never gave it a thought. Well now she would just have to revive them again. She had to use her magic cantrip and allow some time for them to get back to normal. This having been accomplished she introduced them all to the Mac clan and they had a feast and drank mead and the SMA preformed dances and other amusing acts that kept the Mac clan amused and laughter could be heard from the village for miles around via echo's. At dawn the SMA got ready to leave and said fond farewells to all the Mac's who invited them to come whenever they wanted to again and stay as long as they wished. With that they thanked them all again and began their single file march to the tune of HO, HO, HO, HEE, HEE, HEE. A

WEE CLAY JUG OF MEDE HAVE WE, until they were out of sight.

The Mac clan decided to go fishing on the rafts and see if they could catch anything different than what they usually caught. Cor warned them to stay away from the coral atoll today as she had a strange and uneasy feeling that it was not safe over there. The whole clan went off to wave goodbye and wish them good catches and a safe return. Nine rafts left the beach with two men on each. The children played and made sand objects that resembled butterflies and fish, and then they had a competition to see who could build the biggest house. All the adults took the opportunity to laze in the sun and then have a picnic lunch that they had prepared at home. Later that afternoon they saw two rafts coming back and they were full of fish. These were the type that they dried for use in the winter months. Just a little while later they saw another raft returning and one man was standing waving and shouting but no one could hear because of the waves crashing against the nearby rocks.

Cor ran back to the village and told the watch to blow the alarm call on the horn of plenty uses, she was hoping that the rafts further out would hear it and return immediately.

When the two got back to the beach they told Cor that a mohound devil thing had come up out of the sea, it had a huge pointed head and large eyes and long things that must be arms because it took two rafts with them and pulled them down. They said that this was a monster from the deep and had at least eight of these strange long arms with suckers on each one.

Cor knew from ancestral wisdom that the ancients used to call them the black dye monsters and that if they got hold of you, you would never survive. She called on her two goddess advisors Blithe and Mitzion, and also on her great bear protector Ursa. They came at once and she told them what was going on. Ursa told her that when this creature from the deep appeared then they know that the sea God Poseidon was very angry. He said that they can expect more danger from the sea and that this God was very powerful and there were very few Gods that would oppose him. Mostly he has to be challenged by another God but so far none have ever volunteered. Cor decided to call all those related to Poseidon to come up on to the beach and have a meeting with her. Being Gods they knew just what Cor had in mind. Only one God came to meet her and that was the brother of Poseidon, the famous and very powerful God Zeus. Zeus was waiting for a favourable opportunity but one never emerged. Now he finally had a chance to overpower his brother and gain control of the sea. He would go and see what had made Poseidon so angry, and if he could anger him even more he would, and then the fight for the THANE GOD OF THE SEA would be on.

When Zeus met his brother he asked what was making him so angry, and learnt that there was going to be a huge move of the tectonic plates under the sea. That meant that there would be chaos everywhere and there was nothing he could conjure to stop it as the Great Spirit Wathemera had made a decision to demonstrate his power over all of his universal creation. Then Zeus understood Poseidon's frustration and his consequent anger. He now knew that this was not a reason for a challenge but asked if he could join him in trying to convince Wathemea to change his mind.

He welcomed his brother's support and together they went to the pinnacle of the universe using the violet flame of transmutation. When they got there they found a great assembly of ancestral spirits that was on the same mission. However Wathemera would not change his mind and there was a great rumbling, crunching and grinding noise coming from the planet earth. The entire assembly returned and hovered over the earth watching the catastrophe taking place down there.

The waves were huge and very rough with the foaming tops looking just like wild white horses galloping over the Bens, Braes and Trossachs, the sea went over them all and then there was an almighty thundering resonating echo throughout the universe as the two great tectonic plates heaved spasmodically against each other and rent the earth apart. A section of the extended earth and rock separated from the main continent due to the seismic vibration. This section became known as an island, and that is exactly where Cor and the clans were living. This then became their Caledonia as Cor had previously named it. This was the beautiful isle of the Mac clan, and all the other people that were not related to the Mac's who migrated there from the other mainland over the following decades with many risings and wanings of the moon.

The island was not spared from yet another huge quake that left a deep gorge from which large megaliths were thrown into the air and landed all over the Braes and Trossachs scattered apart in all directions. When the vibrating, rumbling and grinding stopped Cor and the clans went to see what devastation had occurred during this chaotic event. Then Cor saw the megaliths she had a sudden yearning to assemble them and make a place of worship to Wathemera. Not far from the gorge was a brae with a flat summit that would be ideal for the purpose that she had in mind. Cor informed theclans of what she intended to do with all the large megaliths and other flat stones that were flung from the gorge as if for a specific purpose. They all thought that she had a very good and acceptable idea. With the mutual agreement of the clan Cor set about the construction of a megalithic monument of the stones arranged in a circle. She was the only one capable of this gigantic task.

This would be the henge from within the circle that they would worship the Great Spirit Wathemera.

Cor went into a state of altered consciousness and then started the chant of levitation. One by one she levitated and placed the megaliths in a circle and put the flat stones on the top also by the mode of levitation. When it was completed it was indeed the most impressive structure on the Isle. Cor said that she would name it at a later date but for the moment it would be known to the clans and others as the place of worship to the Great Spirit.

Chapter 16

Cor told them to lay down prostate and thank Wathemera for sparing their lives during the great upheaval of land and sea. This they all did and the Goddesses Blithe and Mitzion appeared followed by the great protector Ursa. They started to chant with Cor, first the chant of atonement and then the chant of praise to the great spirit followed by the chant of grateful thanks for all the abundant blessings that they received daily from him. Suddenly there was a respectful growl from Ursa and he bowed down in recognition of the apparition of Wathemera. He could only be seen and heard by the Thane spirits of Ursa, Blithe, Mitzion, and Cor. They immediately entered the revered state of altered ethereal status. This was necessary in order to converse with their creator. The Great Spirit called out to them and told them that he was pleased with this construction and also for dedicating it specifically for worship to him. He said that because of her faithfulness to him he would allow Cor to perform many healings there and that this would remain a centre for healing for eternity. Then he handed Cor a list written on a textured substance known only to be used in the heavenlies by his Archangel Raziel for the recording of commandments and the other specifics of the deep and hidden secrets not known to anyone in creation. On this list were the things that Wathemera decreed must be done to live a life acceptable to him. Anyone achieving these instructions would be a person worthy of eternal life in the utopian paradise that awaited them. Then Wathemera said "so is it written, so let it be done" he then gave each of them his blessing and disappeared from sight and sound.

After this experience they all felt rejuvenated and ready to tackle anything that annoyed or opposed them. Life in the village went on peacefully and happily until one day they will never forget. The river that ran into the sea filled up and overflowed into the gorge because of another tectonic plate shift, and a rush of sea water that caused this to happen. That morning at dawn the young clan's men decided to go for a swim in the newly created lagoon. Everyone decided to have breakfast there and challenged the young men to catch fish with their hands, no nets could be used. They all got into the water and started grouping around. The younger lads were just fooling around, splashing and diving in and out just having fun. Suddenly there were deafening screams and the lads got out of the water. Cor went to see what had caused all the commotion, and could not believe her eyes. The water had changed colour, it was now blue-black and there was a huge monster with eight arms holding a man in each one and thrashing them about in the water. She knew this was the monster from the deep sea that had got into the lagoon because of the high tides.

Cor had to do something to help the poor young men that were caught in its mighty grip before it dived back into the abyss and they were lost forever. Cor did the chant of petrifaction and aimed her laser beam that came from her third eye straight at the creature. Instantly it was encrusted with a stone glaze and it could not move it was petrified by the cantrip spell that she cast on it, and so it would remain forever. She removed the cantrip from each of the men that had been caught in the mighty strong grip of the suction cups that were on all the appendages. They were assisted by Cor to free themselves from the worst experience of their lives. They then asked her permission to go to the magnificent stone place of worship, as they wanted to thank Wathemera for rescuing them from the clutches of the monster of the lagoon. Cor gave them permission and they ran off faster than they had ever run before.

The next morning when they had not returned from the monument the clan went off to see what had happened to them. They found them in a trance like state sitting between the megaliths contemplating the direction of the rest of their lives. The clan were relieved to find them alive and well, and Cor told them not to disturb them while they were in a state of such deep meditation.

The clan went home and it was sunset before all the young men returned. They still had a dazed look in their eyes and Cor knew instantly that they had an encounter with the spirit realm. After they had all eaten the young men asked for permission to address the gathered clans. Cor gave her consent, and one by one they took their turn to tell what had been revealed to them. There were only four men that had escaped the grinding jaws of death. The first one's name was Jonah Mac Namara, and the Great Spirit had revealed the name of another huge fish to him. This fish also lived in the deep waters of the sea and it must now be known as the WHALE, he said that it was gigantic and could swallow many things in one gulp including humans and other animals and fish. The second mans name was Octave Mac Donald, and the name of the lagoon monster was revealed to him. It must now be known as OCTAPUS it is a cephalopod mollusc with eight sucker bearing tentacles that were used to grab and hold the food, it then pushed it into its beak like mouth and consumed it. These tentacles were also used to move in the water or on the bottom of the sea-bed. The third man was Jock Mac Cloud and he told them that there would be many more great quakes from the sea as the tectonic plates were going to move periodically, the Bens would also be shaken and many would split. He also said that there would be many icy periods and even the water would freeze in the lochs, and the sea would have a thick barrier of ice that would join one land to the nearest other land mass. This would allow many other strangers to migrate and the earth would be populated by the other hybrid beings. He also told them to harvest the crops and store them, pick and preserve all the fruit, nuts, and berries. They must hunt more often and dry the meat of animals and fish in large quantities as this winter was going to last for many seasons, not just the usual one. The last one was Joseph Mac Carty and he told them that on a far distant planet the Great Spirit had created the beings known as the immortals. These males could never die but live as strong young warriors for eternity.

The only way that they would die is if the head was severed from the body by the sword of another immortal. The creator allowed animosity to build up in each, so that they would always be on the alert. They knew that they would have to fight to the death and the winner would live to fight yet another immortal. This would go on until there was only one and he alone would reign as the immortal king on earth. He would live to witness the end times, when the creator decided to change life on earth into another form. All the immortals would be released from their planetry prison when the ice was thick and the sea froze and ice Bens would be seen from distant horizons. They would be sent in different directions, each determined never to encounter another, for as long as possible, yet knowing that it was inevitable. The clans were stunned into silence and then Cor spoke and ordered them to go with her and all the other sharminniac female healers to the henge to give praise and thanks to Wathemera for all the information and the knowledge about the coming seasons of frozen land and water.

Chapter 17

That night Cor was awakened by the deep friendly growling of her animal spirit protector. When she sat up in her bed he was there standing at his full height just outside her door. Ursa had come to tell her that it was time for her to marry and bear children that could carry on the traditional healer female position as the Thane Sharminn of all the clans. She was shocked and told Ursa that she had never given marriage a thought. "Tell me my beloved protector just who is there among the clans males that I should choose? Thinking of it I can honestly say that there is no one that I think I will be able to live with and bear his children! No! definitely not! So you will just have to choose one for me, now tell me who, what is his name?" "Oh no my precious lassie there is no one here that is good enough for you. The man you marry must have an equal status to yours. He hails from the island of the immortals and when the seas freeze over he will be one of those that choose this direction." "But dear Ursa if there are a few headed in this direction how will I know which one he is?" "I have already chosen him for you and when he arrives he will have an arrow embedded in his left shoulder, and you will have to remove it, that is how you will know who he is my lassie" "You see I have arranged with Sagittarius the cosmic star hunter to shoot the arrow. One could say that I have asked him to play the part of a cupid in your life. This arrow is the beginning of an undying love between the two of you and you will both know the joy of such a union, this is a Devine promise to you. I have also asked Sagittarius to guide your hunters to the herds and assist them in bringing back many carcases for drying purposes before the big freeze. He is a wonderful friend to have and now he will also be on call for you both, for whatever your need may be. Farewell and remember that I am always with you" Cor went to the stone-henge monument to meditate and ask Wathemera for inspiration and wisdom. Then she returned to the village and spent the remainder of the day contemplating her future with this immortal man that she was going to meet.

The following morning a crofter-peasant riding astride a cuddy-donkey came along herding 10 grice-pigs and stopped to ask if they would like to trade with him. He offered a pig for its weight in grain. Cor heard the commotion that the children were making and went out to see what the reason for it was. When he told Cor what he wanted she told him to get away with the grice as the Great Spirit had forbidden them to eat the flesh of swine. She wacked the cuddy on the rump and off it went at an even trot. Then she called all the children and told them never to talk to strangers as they might just be the shape-shifting mohound devils trying to trick them. They have been known to take children back to the underworld of Idiomia and eat them alive. That was enough to make the children run home and hide whenever they saw someone that they did not know. Cor was assured that the children would be safe from those evil beings, and she breathed a sigh of relief.

It seemed as though the ancestors had another lesson they wanted the children to learn and early the next day the clan heard the Kae-jackdaws calling to each other in the forest. Cor warned the children that the call of the Kae meant trouble, and they must be on the look out for any Kae that flew near or around them because they collected things that they wanted and took them to their nests and that thing would be lost forever. They listened attentively to what Cor told them then went off to play. As the time passed the children were experimenting with various things to make games that they could play. They drew lines in the sand and used them to jump over, and then squares to hop into on one foot, then they gathered small sticks and put them in an upright bundle on the ground and let them go. They had to pick up a stick without disturbing any on the others. If one stick dislodged another and it rolled the game would be over and another child got a chance. The winner was the one with the most sticks in his or her hand and got a larger portion of sausage-pudding. As the game ended they saw a wee lassie playing by herself and went to see what she was doing. She was Maggie Mac Dewar and she had taken her bright amulet protector stone out of the pouch that hung around her neck and was rolling it around with some other small pebbles. The oldest lad told her never to do that with her protector amulet it must never be removed from the pouch, and the pouch must never be removed from around the neck. Just as she was going to put it back a Kae swooped down and tried to grab the bright stone with its claws, but missed. Maggie was thankful but the Kae was mad with rage, and made a circle turn in the air and came back and spitefully pecked off the tip of her little nose. Injury received lesson learned by all, Cor felt sorry for her as she was only three years old so she healed her and she got a new tip back on her nose.

At the midnight hour when the village was quiet and all were sound asleep a Todd-fox came in and curled up next to little Maggie on her bed, covering her with its beautiful fluffy tail. Instinctively she put her arm around it and the two slept peacefully all night. When Maggie's mother saw this she sent for Cor. As she stood at the foot of the bed Cor smiled and said that this was a sign from the spirit realm and she must be allowed to keep Todd because he had been sent as her animal spirit protector.

Chapter 18

Cor was preoccupied with her own thoughts about the immortal that was chosen to be her betrothed. She was sitting on a large rock next to the rindle-rivulet with her feet in the water. It was flowing slowly over them giving her a sense of calm and comfort. Some Kelpie-water spirits appeared and they were singing the loe-love song as they happily skipped along on the top of the water. Cor was only slightly aware of a word here and there but five words stuck in her mind and she found herself humming the loe tune often from that moment on, but vocalising the five words "a wonderland at night" "I wish that I knew what this immortal looks like," she said aloud, and there was a voice that came from the base of the rock. "Now, now, my dear lassie patience is a virtue, and virtue is a grace, you will just have to wait for Devine timing as you well know" Cor looked down to see who was giving her the Thane of the clan this advice, although as it correctly said, she knew it anyway.

To her surprise and joy it was her old friend Massassuga the snake that had protected her in the sagacity lodge on the night of her great victory over the previously self-elected and ruling healer males. "Oh! Massassuga it is you, it is wonderful to see you again, come up here and give me a hug, as I could do with one right now" he smiled and hissed and rattled and slithered up onto the rock and wrapped himself around Cor, and they had a memorable reunion. They chatted for a while about the past events in their lives since that day and then Massassuga said "Now it is time to tell you the reasons for coming to you Cor, beside the fact that I was missing you very much"

"When I was slithering past a burn-stream I noticed many blastie-dwarfs splashing in it and washing the dirt off themselves. Then I heard them mention your name so I stopped to eaves-drop my dear. However I was just in time to see some Mohounds and their conspirators the Moloch's shape-shifting into blastie-dwarfs, and unbeknown to them they mingled and heard everything that they had to say. Actually they learnt as much as I did about the comings and goings of the Mac clan, and that angered me into retaliation mode. I silently slithered down into the stream and gave them a snake bite to remember with extra strong venom. All the impostors being in their present form of personification were poisoned and sank to the bottom of the stream where they drowned." He laughed and said "talk about double jeopardy for the shape-shifters, ha! so glad that I could oblige my dear"

"Thank you my treasured and loyal friend, I wish that you could live here with us forever and give up the wandering lonely life" to which he answered "Be careful what you wish for Cor as your wish might just come true. Actually that is the other reason that I came, I wanted to ask your permission to live here with you and the clan as the winter will soon be upon us and I do not fancy living under frozen ground." "Yes you are very welcome Massassuga, and I have been forewarned that this winter will not only be for one season but for many seasons, so I thank Blithe and Mitzion for guiding you here to us"

"Now my dear Cor I want to tell you what I overheard when the evil conspirators were making arrangements to avenge the dearly departed poisoned members of their tribes. That putrid smelling Thane Mohound had been informed by a Moloch member that he had overheard a conversation between Ursa and Sagittarius about shooting an arrow into an immortal indicating that he was the chosen one for you. He said that he had sought a solution from the Carline-witches and that they told him that they would send another man with the same injury ahead and he would also be able to bewitch you to fall in love with him. That way everything would go wrong and the Mohound sagacity would triumph over the Devine wisdom in what would be the biggest laugh of all. So that is the main reason that I have come to you. Remember not to make the error of falling in love with the first wounded one as he is the impostor. No matter how handsome and charming he is you must avoid his advances at all cost Cor. Rather send one of your Sharminn healing females to help the first one. Do not even look at him. Should he want to stay here for the winter just refuse and tell the Sharminn attending to him to send him on his way. But why should I worry, I will be here anyway and another squirt of extra poisonous venom will be just the thing, I am at your service and willing to oblige"

Chapter 19

Cor was very grateful to Massassuga and it was very comforting to know that he was staying, not only for her good but for the good of the clan, as well as for his own protection from the big freeze that would soon start making its appearance. He was reliable and loyal and the perfect one to have on your side as he could get in most places unnoticed and he had his own secret weapon, his powerful and deadly venom. Cor made a special space in her own house available for Massassuga,

It was near the hearth and she put a very thick and comfortable Todd-fox fur down there for him to coil himself up on. As for feeding him, there was no problem because Massassuga lived on mice, rats, moles, voles and other little destructive animals. In actual fact he brought another blessing with him, because he kept all those little creatures away from the precious winter storage of grain, seed, and legume, dried fruits and berries cave. The dried meat and fish and all the dried pelts, furs, and hides were also kept in there. Massassagua became the protector of the winter storage hoard and he would not let anything nor anyone go near the well concealed entrance. The clan called him a guardian angel in disguise. Massassauga had yet another skill to his many attributes, he was able to change the colour of his skin in order to blend in with the surroundings that he was in and therefore could remain undetected anywhere and at anytime.

Cor was lying on her back on the soft green grass looking up at the night sky as she often did while meditating. For some reason she could not keep her gaze off the star sign Gemini. No matter how hard she tried, and she kept on getting a vision of herself with someone. Usually she had no trouble with earthly and spiritual things, but on some occasions Wathemera kept secrets hidden from her.

She tried to understand this strange feeling that had suddenly come over her, that made her burst into tears and cry, she felt as though her heart had split in two. Cor always had sadness in her heart whenever she meditated and always felt alone, even if she was in the midst of a crowd of people.

Lately this feeling had intensified and she felt it constantly. No matter how hard she tried she could not find the reason for it, and now that she had burst into tears for something that she could not understand, she decided to consult her spirit guides. She called on the Goddesses Blithe and Mitzion to come and explain why she felt like this.

They came to her and told her that Wathemera said that they were not to reveal the secret to her until she cried and the tears flowed like a stream from her eyes. Then it would be the great spirits Devine time for the revelation. They told her that her attraction to the Star Gemini was because it was the sign of twins, and she was one. Her mother died giving birth and there was only one wet nurse available, her milk had almost dried up and she never had enough to feed two babies. The nursing mother choose Cor and her twin was given to another wet nurse from a distant clan, that is why they were not raised together. The clan was small and most of them were old when the twins were born, now the last of them had departed to the spirit world and her twin was all alone. However she had the same extrasensory perception as Cor and the same loneliness was always in her heart, now was the Devine timing for the two of them to be able to communicate telepathically. They told her that her twin was in the same state of despair and that she must now concentrate on contacting her and guiding her path to the Mac clan. Mitzion said "do not worry my lovely lassie as she has a companion, and Ursa the great is also her protector as she was born under the same star just minutes after you" "Do you know her name?" "Yes her name is Astra meaning star, but as you were born first you were named Cor which as you know means the brightest star in the constellation of Ursa the Great Bear" Cor was so surprised and so happy that she kept on crying, but now they were tears of joy and great expectations. "just one more thing I would like to know please, who is her companion?" "Well now you are just going to have to wait and see as we are not allowed to reveal it to you as it is a surprise for someone else!" "Oh!

thank you both for coming and for the wonderful surprise, I just hope Astra will get here soon, and her companion is also very welcome here with the Mac clan. Good-bye my beloved guides until we meet again"

Chapter 20

That night Cor and Massassuga were sitting next to the hearth and Cor told him everything that had happened to her since their last conversation. He uncoiled himself slightly, just enough to be able to look into her eyes. He had a sleepy dreamy look in his own eyes and said to her "Well fair lassie then you will have to stop wasting time and get on with that magnetic power you have with the law of attraction. You know that the big freeze is on the way my dear, I can feel a chill in the air and we do not know how far she has to travel, and how many problems she may encounter. Now I have given you the best advice that I can, please act on it." Then he coiled himself up again and went to sleep with a contented smile on his face. Cor started the chant of Telepathy visualising another female who most likely resembled her in every way. She began to hear the far off sound of a tune that she recognised and the closer it got the clearer it became. Oh! Yes it is the loe-love song of the kelpie-water spirits and then she heard the words, a wonderland at night. Suddenly she could also see what looked like herself walking and singing, and then Cor knew that it was Astra. At least they were in contact now and Cor could tell her how to get to the Mac clan, with that thought still in her mind she saw her twin lift her arm up and wave to her and then she blew kisses to Cor. Who returned the action with a big smile on her face. Then the vision and the sound faded and vanished as quickly as it had come.

When Massassuga woke up she told him what had happened, and he was very pleased about the contact that she had, had with Astra. But there was a puzzled look on his face and he hissed out in an angry tone, "Did you notice anything about the surrounding country side? Did you recognise where she is Cor? Then we can judge how far she still has to go!" "No the vision only lasted a few seconds and I only saw her and nothing else, next time I will take notice and if I only see her again with no indication of where she is then I will have to ask my guides for their help again" Just as she said that she suddenly got a contact from Astra, and it frightened Cor. Astra said that she was in danger as the ground in front of her went no further. There was a deep gorge and as far as she could see there was just water everywhere. Astra also said that there was so much molten lava flowing into the gorge and then into the sea that she was sure that she would never get passed but have to go back and try to find another way around. Now Cor knew that she was near the old village that they had to vacate because of the quake and the mighty explosion out of the top of the Ben. She told Astra not to worry as she would send her loyal and trustworthy friend Massassuga to her as he knew the way very well.

He would do anything for Cor and now added Astra to his very short list of close friends, off he went slithering at his top speed, in the direction of the old village. He knew that the moon would rise and wane many times before he reached her, so he never stopped except to hunt for food and have a drink of water now and then. His journey seemed to have no end, it just went on and on and he was very tired. He was contemplating a short rest and just have forty winks while he rested, but at that moment there was a breeze coming from the direction in which he was headed. He stopped and sensed that there was a delicate scent wafting in the breeze. Was he dreaming, was he slithering along in his sleep, or did he remember that scent from way back in his younger days, he wondered.

Then he heard a rustling in the long thatch grass and with the sound came that fragrant scent of the female of his species. Massassuga almost fainted, not only from exhaustion, hunger and thirst but from the memories that had returned to him from his long gone youth. He stood up on his tail so that the full length of his body gave him a (one could say, birds eye view) over the grass. There she was Astra at last, but what was coiled around her. It was her life long companion Iris the rainbow shaded messenger snake that had alerted Massassuga's sensory glands moments ago, he could not believe his luck. The Gods are also on my side he thought, as he winked at the moon.

Chapter 21

After the introductions Astra recommended that he rests for the night and that they would commence their journey at dawn. So Massassuga slithered along leading the way, and Iris decided to join him so the two chatted about their long lonely lives and the events leading up to their happy meeting. When they had one brae-mound to go over before they reached the forest, Cor appeared on the summit and then came running along and Astra did the same. The twins hugged each other and laughed and cried while their life long companions looked on. Then they went on through the forest and into the Mac clan village. Everyone had gathered and a huge feast had been prepared and a vat of mead was opened for the celebrations. That night the twins and their companions stayed in Cor's house. The next day the clans men started to build a house for Astra as all the houses were small unless they had an extended family, then they were enlarged accordingly.

Astra told Cor that the earthquake that had caused what Cor had named Caledonia to be rent apart from the main continent, also caused a lot of damage in other parts of that great continent. This massive part of earth was known as "Avalonia". It was a section of two other land-masses known as "Atlantis, and Lemuria." (Lucy Cavendish-The Lost Lands). Astra said that during her Astral travels in the cosmos she had encounted many other civilizations in the inter-galactic universe. The constellations that she had visited were very well advanced and she had gained much wisdom through her contact with them. The ones that she had contact with were the Orion, who had killed his lover Diana, she had heard many stories from him especially the hunting ones as that is his field of expertise, she also visited his star Rigel.

In the north she had been to Ursa their own protector, and Leo minor, to Andromeda the chained lady, Valpecula, and Cassiopeia. Then she went south again near Orion and visited Dorado, Lupus, Hydrus, Centaurius, and Monoceros. However she wanted to go north and visit Draco. As they Cor and Astra are Dragonfae, which are a group of beings that are part Dragon, part fae, part Angel and part mer-being. Actually they are hybrid beings that are part earthly, and part galactalic and have the best of both traits.

Astra said that she had been informed that there would be great volcanic eruptions as the God Vulcan was jealous of the progress of the other Gods and was going to take vengeance with molten Lava. Explosions from the summit of the Bens would cause rivers of lava to flow, and that this would take place periodically. Also that the great tectonic plates would shift due to lava pressure under the sea and the quakes would again cause havoc. She told Cor that her informant wished to remain anonymous. The great continents of Atlantis and Lemuria would be known as lost lands, and that the Atlanteans would bring about the downfall of Lemuria. However Avalon would be spared for many eons, until the Great Spirit Wathemera made a decision in his own Devine time, and no one knew what it was or when it would be.

Cor was fascinated by all this new information and told Astra that she never had the urge to go on an Astral travel. She said that she always chanted and called to the Great Spirit, and the goddesses, as well as their beloved protector Ursa and they always came at once. Astra said "Yes I know that is what you did before but you had to wait for us to meet first as Wathemera knew that you were much more capable to lead and teach the beings that he was going to create than I am. That is why you and I had to meet in his Devine timing. Together we are very powerful and he will need us both to help the light-beings here on earth. The only difference is that he will call us and send us into the inter-galactic spheres whenever the occasion calls for it, and the spirits will still come when we need them, for whatever purpose. Then Cor asked Astra the question that she needed an answer to.

"My dearest twin when you were on one of your travels did you perhaps just happen to see the Island Planet that holds the Immortal men within its boundries. Until the big freeze they will not be able to leave it?" "No dear sister those are deep and hidden secrets as you well know, bide your time and you will soon have the revelation that Watherema told Blithe and Mitzion to guard.!"

Chapter 22

An unexpected visit from their goddesses brought such joy to the twins; they had never come without being called or because they needed to warn them about something. Here they both were but they looked concerned, and then told the twins that they must go together and travel in the cosmic universe as they had much to learn from the beings the Pleiadians and the Sirians. They would receive further travel instructions once they had completed this command.

Cor was not very keen to go as she had very strange feelings, there was an aching in her loins and also her breasts that she had never experienced before. Then there was this unquenchable desire that she had in her heart, and she knew that it was a longing to fill the void that she felt she had become.

When she discussed this all with Astra she told her that she would have to go with her as it was a command from the

Great Spirit sent to them by their Goddesses, and that she knew they would be very angry if she did not obey.

Cor knew this was true she did not have to be told and was upset with her twin for chiding her. However she then decided to go with but had an in depth conversation with Astra about her feelings. Astra said that she also had those feelings she understood the yearning for something but she did not know what it was. The winter was starting and they both knew that the big freeze was on the way. This worried them both as they would have to leave the clan and the entire village protected only by the Sharminn and the warlords. Cor invited Astra to accompany her to the Henge of stone to worship and praise Watherema. This they did together and were surprised by the appearance of Blithe and Mitzion again. They were told by them that they would be in the village and stay in the houses of Cor and Astra but be incognito. They would also be invisible to all but the Sharminn healing females who would be informed as to why they were there. Relieved and with the blessings of their goddesses the twins took off into the universe.

They went to the seven star system known as the Pleiades which is in the constellation of Taurus.

These beings are human like and have a very beautiful third eye that is decorated to almost entrance a being with a lesser status, if gazed upon. They are beautiful intelligent beings and are particularly talented in music, dance, and song. There we learnt that they share a similar cellular matrix as the yet to be created humans but were attuned to a much higher frequency, and were very advanced in the use of holograms and laser technology. They had also developed hyper space travel and were capable of going anywhere that they desired. However Wathemera had commanded that a number of them would be sent to earth to inter-mingle with the humans, once they were placed on the planet Gaia. This was so that the humans would be able to reactivate their dormant DNA, but it would only come to pass in the distant future, and many hybrid humans would hold office in a very high capacity.

From there we went to Sirius, and learnt that they were masters of time travel, and were able to transmit information without embellishment. They can describe hidden worlds but are only allowed to do so in Devine timing. Sirius is the galactic university and has more professors than any other cosmic system. They are very advanced in metaphysics and this is the place that the ascended masters often travel to. They told us that Sirius has a direct link with the solar system of planet earth, and will be in contact with the first civilizations to be known as the ancients. These will be mighty nations and records of their existence and secret magical wonders will be kept in well hidden places, until the Devine timing takes action. The linear time would change on mother earth and there would be an interwoven time and dimension system introduced. Then there would be advanced psychic and galactic consciousness and the beginning of a new 5,125 year energy would begin on the planet. The genesis of the fifth world would begin in the year 2012 A.D.

The twins were expecting their next instruction soon, and when it came it was one that they had both hoped for. They were commanded to return to earth and the Mac clan village.

Chapter 23

Whenhen they arrived there was a very deep layer of snow all over the Bens, Braes, Trossachs, and the village rooftops were all covered in dense layers of snow. Massassauga and Iris had detected them through their powerful sensory glands. They both slithered at great speed to welcome them home.

When they were near enough they threw themselves at their beloved companions coiling around them and rubbing their heads against Cor and Astra's ears. "Hello treasured companions we are so pleased that you are home" they said. "We have something to show you" they both voiced together, and uncoiling themselves they slithered to Astra's house. The twins followed them and when they got inside they were surprised to see Massassuga and Iris standing up at full length with a coy look on their faces. Then they parted and went down on to the floor again forming a circle around the Todd-fox fur that was Iris's bed. "Look said Massassuga we are about to become parents" Sure enough there were six eggs in a cluster right in the centre of the Todd-fox fur. The twins were ecstatic and asked if they could cradle the eggs for just a wee while. "OH yes please do these babies must get used to you and your touch," said Iris. Cor and Astra got so much pleasure and joy out of holding these eggs, that they almost forgot to greet the clan.

Little did they know that Blithe and Mitzion had told the clan that the twins were on their way, so they prepared a great welcome feast and opened a vat of the precious mead. They had a double celebration, one to welcome the twins and one to welcome all the new born babies that had arrived during their absence, and then Massassuga coiling himself around Iris announced that they would soon be parents. Everyone clapped their hands and a happy "YEA, YEA," sounded throughout the village. Then Blithe and Mitzion said their farewells and returned to their spirit abode.

The Sharminn and warlords gathered around the twins to give a report on all the events that had taken place. They told of another violent shaking of the earth and also of another mighty explosion from the Ben that had many layers of snow covering it, and it had hardened into solid ice. The two snakes rattled and hissed to show their disapproval. Mac Tavish reported that the storage cave was warm and dry and had been kept free of all vermin by the loyal slitherers.

Cor asked if the big freeze had turned the sea water into thick hard ice yet, and the answer was somewhat disappointing. Yes it had started along the coastline all around the Isle but had not reached out to the deep sea as yet.

The twins felt melancholy and could not even smile." What is wrong with the two of you, you are acting as though you are at deaths door," asked the Mac Nab "Surely you can not expect us to be cheerful all the time they replied simultaneously" He was not satisfied with such a lame excuse, so off he went to the Sharminn healing female, and asked them all to come to his aid, as he was sure that there was something ailing the twins. They went immediately and examined them then with a smile on their faces, told the clan that it was nothing to worry about. They fabricated a deceiving answer, as they all knew that it was a personal matter and it must remain private. They told the clan that the twins were just very tired from their extended journey through the universe, and that the mood that they were in would pass as soon as they had gained their strength.

The real reason was a very different story, the one neither could explain, they could only tell their twin how they felt, and sympathise, and comfort each other. At least they knew that these feelings would end when the Immortal males arrived, as they thought, from over the ice from the Island that had held them captive for so long. This yearning, longing, aching, hunger that left them feeling a void that they thought could never be filled. It was an endless pining that caused them to feel that their hearts had broken. They both went up to the henge to worship and praise Wathemera, and to beg him to end this suffering if it be his Devine will. They both lay prostate and in silent meditation for the duration of the night hours, feeling the iciness of the big freeze but ignoring it.

Chapter 24

When they arrived back in the village they were surprised to see that the blastie-dwarfs had returned

The thane leader asked Cor if they could stay for the day as they had been called by the Great Spirit to return to their home star. This is the Dwarf star that is very far away and relatively small with low luminosity. They were commanded to wait until the vesper star appeared then the violet flame of transmutation would take them home. However they said that a number of them had to remain to ensure that their cellular matrix would be transmitted to other humanoids through the consummation of marriage. These blasties had remained in another district that had been chosen by the Great Spirit himself. By now the ice sheets had almost covered most of the visible sea and the cold weather was unbearable unless they stayed indoors. Those that had to go to the storage cave to get supplies, had to wear extra thick furs, and make sure that their faces were protected from the direct wind. This resulted in having to walk backwards on most days, and was most unpleasant indeed.

The emergence of the vesper star was now clearly seen in the sky above the Mac village and right next to it the violet flame started the descent to planet earth. It was so beautiful to watch, and as it got brighter and closer the melodious sound of celestial voices could be heard. Cor told everyone to go to the henge as that is where the transmutation would take place. Astra and Cor accompanied the blasties and watched them go safely up in the magnificent violet flame; they gave thanks to Wathemera for their safe return, and promised that they would always be welcome at the village.

They had hardly removed the extra fur covering, when there was a loud banging on the door. The night watch stood there almost frozen stiff and Cor told him to come inside. "What are you doing here, and why have you left your post unguarded?" asked Cor "I respectfully beg your pardon Cor but the horn of plenty uses will not make a sound anymore, and as there is someone approaching I thought it best to warn you in person" "Thank you very much you made the right decision, could you see who it is that is on the way/" "Yes it is a man on his own and it looks as if he is wounded by the way that he is walking" "Thank you for the information I will send a Sharminn healer female to attend to him, and contact Cornucopia for advice about the function of the horns sound"

Sure enough it was the first wounded man that Cor had been warned about, and the Sharminn removed the arrow and healed the wound with Cor's magic potion. Then when he asked to stay the Sharminn that had healed him told him emphatically no, and sent him on his way with three very powerful warlords to accompany him past the mear-boundary of the Mac clan village. Now Cor was so excited because she knew that the Immortal men would be arriving soon. However there was another matter of grave importance to attend to and Cor knew that she had to do it immediately.

She asked Astra to accompany her to the henge and chant the tone of spirit communication to Cornucopia as it is very important that they contact her tonight. They both stood in the centre of the henge and chanted loud and clear. She appeared before them and Cor asked her the question concerning the sound that could no longer be made by the horn of plenty uses. "My dear's the horn was deliberately silenced by me, so that the impostor would not be aware that he had been detected before he could knock on your door. Had it have sounded he would have shape-shifted into the form of Massassuga or Iris until he could no longer be seen, and then you would have opened the door with serious consequences. I hope that I have been of acceptable service to you and can assure you both of my assistance at anytime. The horn of plenty will produce its sound again just as before."

"Thank you for your much appreciated help, and the blessing that it gave us." With that having been done the twins went to their own houses and had a bite to eat and a sip of mead in front of the warm hearth, before going to bed. Cor lie in her bed and let her thoughts be only on the arrival of her Immortal man. All the physical feelings that she did not understand returned and with them came the vision of a wounded male making his way through the deep snow toward the Mac village, and then she went to sleep keeping the vision in her sub-conscious mind.

Chapter 25

That night Cor had one dream after the next and some were sweet and some were very frightening.

Most of them were of the past and some were of the future, while she was dreaming she heard the eerie screeching of her ben-side ancestral grandmother, and she knew that it could only mean that there was trouble coming to the village. Cor woke up with sweat running down her face and she was trembling all over and shivering at the same time. She sat up and rubbed her eyes and then she saw her standing next to the bed. "Greetings grandmother, please tell me the reason for your welcome visit" "Oh my beautiful granddaughter I wish that it were glad tidings that I bring, but I am so sorry to be the one to warn you that the Mohounds and their conspirators are on the warpath again. They have convinced the Carline-witches to do a vile and evil thing at their bidding. I am not sure what they have in mind but it is unthinkably evil. I have come to warn you that bad things are going to happen and I think that you must put a guard next to the vats of mead. I have a feeling that they are aiming to use intoxication as a secret weapon. Warn all the clan people not to partake in drinking this precious liquid as I think it will be tainted. I am keeping a watchful eye out for anything untoward and I will inform you if I detect anything. Goodbye and may the blessings of Wathemera be with you all."

Just after dawn the horn of plenty uses sounded the warning of someone approaching, and Cor and Astra rushed out to see what was happening. They were expecting a silent attack of some kind, due to the night visit from their ben-side ancestor. The snow was falling thick and fast and obscured their view. So they ventured further out and away from the village, then they saw a lone figure and went to see if they could assist. On approaching they saw a man with an arrow through his left shoulder and Cor almost fainted, if it were not for the support from her twin she would have fallen down in the snow. The moment that she had longed for had finally come, here was her Immortal man and she gasped and went forward with Astra to help him. They both said "Hello we are here to help you, hold on to us and we will soon have you inside next to a warm hearth." "Oh thank you both so much, I am in a lot of pain and feel as though I have frozen almost solid" At the sound of his voice Cor stuttered something but no words would come other than stt, stt, thank the great spirit that Astra took over the conversation when she realised how just touching this man, had affected her twin. When they got him into Cor's house and next to the hearth they gave him a potion to deaden the pain, and mercifully it put him to sleep. Cor removed the arrow and healed the wound with the healing power given to her by the great-spirit.

Astra levitated him using the power of sound while Cor put a soft thick bear fur down for him to lie on and covered him with another one. The heat from the hearth and the furs warmed him and he slept soundly with the help of the potion that Cor had given him to drink. The twins sat and stared at him for ages then Astra said. "Well my twin this handsome muscular creature is your Immortal man and you must admit that he was well worth waiting for" "You are right sister I would have waited for the rest of my life here on earth if I had to, but thanks to the great spirit for hearing my plea and sending this man to me now in this lifetime" Then Astra said goodbye and went off to her home and hearth.

When she got inside she heard Iris and Massassuga hiss and she went over to where they were.

They greeted her with rattles and smiles, then Iris got off of her fur bed and Lo and behold, her eggs had hatched and there were six tiny babies peacefully sleeping in the fur. Five looked just like their mother and one was identical to the proud father. Astra congratulated them and gave them both a big hug and told them that she could hardly wait to hold the babies. Then she said that she would tell Cor in the morning as she did not want to disturb her now, because her Immortal man had arrived. Massassauga was not going to wait and slithered off home to check him out and give Cor the good news.

He went under the hide covering to the entrance of Cor's house, it was dark except for the glow from the hearth, and silent except for a deep nasal sound indicating that this Immortal was fast asleep. Cautiously he got on the bed and saw that Cor was also sleeping next to the man and wondered if he had performed the rite of union with Cor. He could not sense any vibratory frequency that indicated that there had been a culmination of joy or disappointment neither could he sense any odour indicating that there had been an ejaculation from the male reproductive glands. With a feeling of sadness he went and coiled up on his fur bed, sighed and proceeded to dream of the future. Would Cor still be the Thane leader of the Mac clan and all the other Celt clans that were now joining them through migration from their places of birth? Or would this Immortal man influence her to do things his way? No he knew that Cor was born to lead and was a hybrid of many brilliant ancestral leaders, there were many Gods among them, so he slept peacefully.

Chapter 26

Before sunrise the morning star Venus was visible in the east and Cor could see it from her warm bed, it was twinkling in the darkness, and it seemed to Cor that it was winking at her giving her its approval of the love to come. She could feel the warmth radiating from behind her back and then suddenly remembered the events of the last night. She turned around slowly and looked into the most beautiful blue eyes that she had ever seen. Her Immortal man was awake, and he gave her the most beguiling smile. "Good morning my Angel, thank you for saving me from a freezing night out in the forest, and also for removing the arrow from my shoulder. It was very painful and I knew the wound was infected as it was hot and very red, thank you a million times" "It was my pleasure and also my duty as the thane sharminn and supreme ruler. I am Cor the first reincarnation of my ancestral grandmother, who always comes to tell me of future events that are unacceptable and threatening to our people. What is your name and where is the land of your birth?"

"I am from the Attar Command we are roaming representatives of the Galactic Confederation,(Lucy Cavendish-Lost Lands) and our base moves every century to a new star system. We are intergalactic light workers and a chosen few are immortal. I am an Immortal and I was sent here from the constellation of Aquila in the north. The Lord Ashtar commanded me to this planet to mate and mix my cellular matrix with a hybrid of your exact ancestry. My name is Hawk Mac Allan and I was selected by the Great Spirit to join in union with you." "Oh that is wonderful news; I have been awaiting your arrival for a long time now. I am so happy that you are here. You must be hungry I have some bread and the honey that we collected from the wild bees during the summer months, also would you like a hot brew of herbs that keep one strong and healthy?" "Yes please that will be most satisfying; I will appreciate it very much."

After this delicious meal Hawk stood up and walked to the entrance, he lifted the hide covering and looked out over the sea that was now frozen solid and there was no water to be seen even in the distance. There were dark threatening clouds moving in their direction and he could feel the cold wind as it howled from across the ice, bringing a blizzard that would last for days on end. He turned and said "Where is your storage place, I must go and bring some wood and more thick furs as this cold is going to be the worst in living memory" Cor told him about the storage cave and was so pleased that she would never have to go and do these unpleasant chores now that her precious man was here. She hurriedly sent word to all the clan to stock up now and not wait another hour. Since it was to cold for the watch to stay in the tower, each family had to be alerted. Cor wrapped strips of warm fur around Massassuga and Iris and sent them as her messengers. They went but without a smile.

The howling blizzard was turning the falling snow into ice before it hit the ground, and all the men battled against it trying to get home with the supplies that they had collected.

No one but Cor realized the danger that this brought, she immediately called to mind the warning of her ben-side grandmother, about the unspeakable evil that would be loosed on the Mac clan.

When Hawk returned he found Cor sitting at the hearth with her head to one side, and silent tears were falling as the revelation was finally made to her by Ursa her animal spirit protector.

He stacked the wood against the hide covered entrance to provide more insulation, and put the food parcel down next to it. Hissing and rattling Massassuga managed to slide through the one corner, announcing that they had completed their orders, and Iris had gone home to her babies and Astra.

He was so cold that he could not even bend his long body, so lay stretched out in front of the hearth to thaw as he stuttered out the reason, for not coiling up on his fur.

Now Hawk came over to Cor and took her in his arms, asking why she was crying. She explained that it had been revealed to her that the warning of the evil her ancestor had told her about, was now upon them. She told him that some of the males that had gone to get supplies would never return home. They had been attacked by the shape-shifting Mohounds who had assumed their identity and would replace them through the long icy season. The females would be unaware of the change over and they would mate with them thinking that they were their husbands. It was too late to do anything now and the poor husbands had been taken to the labyrinthine underworld of the mohound sphere of Idiomia. There they would be consumed by the Mohounds as food for the long season.

Cor said that she cried for the men who would lose their lives by being bound and eaten alive, and for their woman who were ignorant of this fact. However she would receive wisdom from the Great Spirit on how to counteract the evil mohound sagacity.

Massassuga had thawed now and had coiled himself up on his fur bed, asleep with one eye open, just to make sure that this Immortal would not harm his beloved Cor in anyway. His mother had told him never to trust strangers, and he never did.

Chapter 27

After having had a warm herb drink Hawk took Cor by the hand and led her to the bed, removing their clothes as they always did when going to bed in those long gone times. Hawk cupped Cor's large firm breasts in his hands and fondled them, while kissing her lips tenderly. Then he picked her up and placed her on the bed and got in next to her pulling the thick soft fur over them. He kissed her all over her body and moved to sit astride her. His appendage was thick, long and throbbing and Cor took it in her hand and with a smile asked "What do you call this appendage of yours and what do Immortal men use it for" she asked "Well it has a duel purpose, the one is to empty the body of excess fluid and the other is for reproduction. However I call it my love muscle, as it is the part of my body that gives me the most pleasure. Will you allow me to demonstrate this to you, as it will also consummate our union. It must enter your female birth canal and at first it will be painful but that won't last for long, then you will experience the most joy that you have ever had in your lifetime this I promise you." Cor gave her consent with a smile on her face and lifting her arms up put them around him and pulled him down on top of her. She felt his love muscle enter her birth canal and made a soft sound indicating that she had felt pain. Then as he started to move rhythmically and verbally express his love for her at the same time, Cor felt a sensation that made her body quiver with delight and she felt his body shudder and with an exclamation of satisfaction he softly whispered "thank you my angel, I love you so very much."

"I love you to and yes that is the most fabulous sensation that I have ever experienced, it has brought me so much joy, and I love you with all my heart. Do the Immortals only partake in that function once in their life time?" "No my darling little angel the Immortals can perform that action as many times as they like, just like any other living thing that the great spirit created. It is our obligation to fulfil his command to procreate" "Oh I was hoping that you would say that, I was worried that Immortals being different to other mortals would have other commands from the Great Spirit. I am sleepy and feel so much peace and contentment now. Please hold me in your strong arms while we sleep" So Hawk took Cor in his arms and with their legs intertwined held her close to his body all night.

The blizzard and the howling north wind bringing more and more icy snow was the reason that the clan members never went out and consequently, only got news about each other when the men went to the storage cave. Cor knew that there was something wrong and had shivers up and down her spine. "Hold me please I know that there is a very frightening thing that I have to face and deal with very soon, and I fear that it has to do with the Mohound devil sagacity, which they have put into practice. Hawk please tell me if there were any men drinking mead in the cave when you went to get supplies?" "Yes there were four that had had too much and were slurring and swaying on their way out with their supplies that kept on falling off their backs. Why do you ask my angel?" "My ben-side ancestor had warned me that the mead would be tainted and no one must drink it now. I told everyone in the village not to but obviously some of them disobeyed my orders, and now I fear the consequences." Hawk reassured her that she had power and the Devine wisdom that she had inherited from her ancestor, Cor the first for whom she had been reincarnated. She knew all that but needed some encouragement occasionally. Now that her male was here a hug and a reassuring kiss toped it all and she went ahead fearlessly with him at her side. He asked Cor if she would now replace the term Female to Woman and Male to Man and she agreed.

Although there were clouds above the village the distant horizon was partially clear and Cor could sense evil all around. She moved the hide covering of the entrance to her home just enough to peep out, and sure enough there was a bad moon rising. This was always an indication of trouble and even though she was expecting it, she never knew just in what form it would come. The moon had circles of fluorescent blood red around it just the same colour as the mohound eyes.

The night after she had seen the bad moon rising she was called by two Sharminn healing woman to come and assist them as they were having difficulty with a woman trying to give birth. Cor went with them to the last house in the village, and could hear a woman screaming from a distance, she could even be heard above the howling north wind. They hurried to her and Cor examined her and said that the baby was too big to pass through the birthing canal and that they would have to chant the chant of mercy to Watherema. While they did that Cor performed a cantrip of magic by pushing her hands into the woman's stomach just above both her hips and splitting it open pulled out not one but two babies. Then she healed the wound and soothed the woman who had undergone so much pain. Cor gave her some healing and pain potion that she had brewed and the exhausted woman gratefully fell asleep.

Now she went over to the healer woman who had been chanting and to her amazement they were both standing with their backs to the twins that had just been born. "Why are they not crying, have they both departed?" "No Cor but be ready for a shock" When she looked at them she saw that they had no gender and this could mean only one thing. They were hybrid creatures that had been sired by a shape-shifter, as they were androgynous. But which of the many cosmic shape-shifting androgynous beings had sired them, that was the question. Cor peeped at the bad moon once again and there she was shown a reflection of the constellation of Andromeda, the lady chained to her chair. This told Cor that this poor woman was abused and tied down and had no choice with the mating. Then one baby opened its eyes and they were entirely fluorescent blood red. Mohound devils she uttered. Then with her nails she removed their eyes and sealed up their eyelids so that they would be blind.

Chapter 28

Cor went home and told Hawk what had just happened. He was shocked and asked her why she had removed the baby's eyes. "Well you see the Mohounds use their eyes to reflect information from anywhere as long as there is one of them present. Now they would have had two innocent informers to go anywhere in the village at their command. The problem is that they do not remain innocent for very long, as soon as they are able to get around they won't wait to be told where to go. These beings will just go where there is anything to report back to the thane mohound on the sphere of Idiomia. That is why I had to make them blind, otherwise no one here on the planet earth would ever be safe, and even their very thoughts would be reflected back". News soon spread that the woman's husband had killed her and the blind babies and that he said that he would eat them all during the big freeze. Cor sprang into action when she heard this news, as she now knew for certain that this was not the woman's husband but a mohound shape-shifting replacement. Accompanied by Hawk she went to the house and was just in time to see him bite into his own off spring. She did the chant of petrifaction, and turned him into solid rock, and then Hawk took the bodies out and buried them where there had once been sea water. When the ice thawed their bodies would be consumed by the huge fish.

Astra went to visit Cor and took Iris and the little ones with her. Massassuga was delighted to see his babies, and his darling Iris. The little ones had grown and were slithering around all over hissing and rattling with such joy whenever they discovered something that amused them. Iris said "We will have to give them names so that they come to us when we call them, don't you think?" Astra replied and said "No that must be done by the lifelong companion to whom Wathemera assigns them, for now an extra long hiss will have to suffice, and they will all come at once." Then Astra was introduced to Hawk and he was dumbfounded by the fact that he would not be able to tell who was who if they were separated from each other. It was a disturbing thought indeed, they were identical, and only they would know if he was with Cor or Astra! Massassuga whispered in his ear

"The only way to tell them apart is to pay attention to her life long companion; you see we know which is which. I am always with Cor and Iris is always with Astra we never leave them, except when they send us on errands, and it seldom happens that they send both of us at the same time."

Hawk was very thankful for this information because Immortals had to remain faithful to only one woman through out her lifetime, and if they disobeyed this order they would be recalled and replaced by another Immortal.

Astra's thoughts of Hawk were troubling her and giving her feelings that she should not have for her twin's man. She discussed this with Iris who advised her to go on an astral travel that would take her mind off of Hawk, and keep him out of her dreams. Unfortunately Iris could not accompany Astra this time because her babies were not old enough to be assigned to a life companion just yet. With her mind made up she decided to go to the constellation of Vulpecular which is in the north of the universe, so she went to say farewell to Cor, Hawk and Massassuga.

They were very surprised that Astra was going to leave during this extra long season of the ice winter. However Cor knew that she would never be able to change Astra's mind once it was made up, so they all said bye-bye and wished her a safe journey.

Astra asked Wathemera to send some angels to accompany her as it was a very long and lonely journey that she had undertaken. She also asked him to let her find a man like Hawk that would love her as much as he loved Cor. She then did the chant for Galactic transmutation and started levitating to where the angels were waiting to meet her. She could see them as she was approaching and noticed that Wathemera had not only sent angels, but had given her the greatest honour by sending Arch Angels as her travelling companions.

Astra waved and shouted "Hello dearest Arch Angels, I praise the great spirit for sending you to accompany me, and

I thank you with all my heart for coming. I am Astra twin of Cor born under the constellation of Ursa Major, and we are privileged to have him as our protector" When she got to them they were singing praises to the great spirit Wathemera, then with wings touching they formed a circle around her and simultaneously said "We welcome you Astra and also send fond greetings to your power spirit protector Ursa the great" Then a trumpet sounded and the Angel Raziel came forward and said "I am Raziel who keeps the secrets of the universe, and this is Michael the leader of the great spirit's army, this is Raphael the spiritual healer angel, this is Ariel who has courage beyond anything and is known as the lioness of the great spirit, this is Haniel who is in charge of the moon cycles and is also sensitive and helps one find love and passion, this is Raguel who brings Devine order into your life, and this is Jeremiel who helps overcome difficulties. We are the ones that were sent to accompany you, other Arch Angels will join us should the need for their specialities arise" Then the trumpet sounded again and Michael came forward to lead the travellers through the cosmos and from one constellation on to the next and then from one galaxy to the next, until they reached their destination of the constellation of Vulpecular.

Chapter 29

Michael turned north and on past the
constellations of Ursa, Lyra, Draco Aquila,
Auriga, Polaris, Lacerta, Delphinus,
Andromeda, and Cassiopeia until at last they reached
Vulpecular.

Ariel was behind Michael as she would soon have to
confront the thane leader, the beings that lived here were
canines and she was the lioness of the Great Spirit the one and
only that had the courage to handle a confrontation should
one occur. If the need arises she will shape-shift into the body
of a lioness and fight her enemy, tooth and claw. However
the presence of Michael at her side and ever ready to use his
sword if the beast that came forward got the better of her was
very comforting.

They landed at the foot of a huge Ben and cautiously
moved around, it appeared deserted and so did the trossachs
that lay ahead. They climbed many Bens and crossed the

trossachs on foot so as to be able to contact these beasts as they could not fly. They walked for many risings and wanings of the moon and one day Haniel said "I am sure that we are very close as I know that the moon cycles will change, but I fear that there will be a bad moon on the rise"

Astra had experienced many bad moons and what ever followed them was always frightening. She turned to Michael and said "Maybe we should leave this constellation and go to another before the bad moon rises." "Raguel came forward and said no we can not do that the Great Spirit sent me along so that Devine order can be brought into your life as an answered prayer." Then Jeremiel came forward and said "Raguel is right and I was sent to help you overcome difficulties so we must go on" then Raziel said "I was sent because I know the secrets of the universe, and if you leave here now then your desperate prayer to find your man can not be answered. You see Astra your man was captured during his travels while he was sleeping, and is held captive here by the beasts that we have to conquer" "Oh dear, thank you for revealing this secret to me now I will never leave until we have found and rescued him." "Do not fear for that is the reason that I was sent, I will fight to the death of every beast that challenges me, and Haniel will see to it that he is your Immortal man as she will bring love and passion into your lives. Now on we go"

Sure enough the moon came out and, yes Haniel was right it was a bad moon, a very bad moon indeed. The red colour was not only all around it but covered it totally, Oh yes a very bad moon.

It seemed that from out of nowhere there came the most blood-curdling and eerie mixture of howling and snarling and roaring and bellowing that any of them had ever heard. Then a loud trumpeting joined in with the other sounds. Now Raziel spoke "This is a mixture of the various species that live in this constellation and there appears to be a battle for the dominance as thane leader. Come quickly to the summit of this Ben and we will watch them fight to the death or until the majority surrender and acknowledge the supremacy of one beast." "Will you tell us all what species they are please Raziel" "Yes I will because the great spirit has given me permission to tell you not only their species but also what is going to happen to them. There will be a fight for the supreme thane leader and then all of them will be transmuted to the planet earth. Wathemera has kept them here until his Devine time and order for this creation to descend to that orb. It will be directly after this battle and we will be here to watch them go, they will not all be sent to the same areas on the planet but to the ones selected by Wathemera. Some will be sent to the north and some to the south, others will go west and the remainder will go east. The climate all over the planet has caused the big freeze as you know and so many will migrate, trying to find better living conditions"

They reached the summit and saw that the battle was taking place in a trossach surrounded by Bens and all the Bens were covered by the beasts that were watching the mighty battle. Only the strongest and most powerful ones were the contenders for the esteemed title.

The first battle that they witnessed was between two huge striped sabre tooth carnivore's, they were tearing each others flesh with their claws and then using their sabres to rip the flesh off the body, standing at full height the one eventually got the other to fall down and then he jumped upon it and sank his huge sabres into its throat and killed it. Although it was very badly wounded it crawled away from the arena and then proceeded to lick all the wounds. Now Raphael the healing angel went forward and miracously healed the victor. Then he went all around looking for the other badly wounded beasts that had fought before our arrival and healed them all.

The last two contenders were the huge mammoths and they were almost the size of a dod-hill on the earth. They entered the arena from north and south and trumpeting and charging they came together with a mighty head butt and started to push against each other trying to get their tusks into the throat of the opponent. The one had a curved tusk and a straight tusk and the other had two straight tusks.

They went around in circles stabbing anywhere that they could reach and blood gushed out of the big gashes, it was spurting into the air and onto the ground and it became obvious that they were getting tired and starting to weaken. Then the one with two straight tusks got one tusk through the curve of the opponents one and pulled and pushed until the straight tusk went right through the other one's eye and into it's brain. The enormous creature collapsed to the ground and with a last trumpet died in a pool of blood.

Then there was lightning and thunder and the noise of all the frightened beasts making their own cries that echoed throughout Vulpecular. A very bright light appeared and it had every colour ever seen intertwined in an awesome variegation. This light spread everywhere until all the beasts were covered and then a mighty wind came and took them all away in a downward direction towards the planet earth that the Great Spirit creator had planned for them. Suddenly there was silence and Raziel said "it is done." Astra spoke and asked. "Dear Raziel everything that you told us has come to pass but where will I find my Immortal man, did you not say that he is held captive here?"

"Yes he is held captive here and now we will look to Haniel who will help you to find him."

"I know where he is being held, it is in a cave with all the little Todd's that were taken captive with him, as he is their thane leader. But they are guarded by very fierce hybrid wolverines that have to keep them captive at all costs. Let us go now" Haniel led them to the cave and at the entrance they were accosted by the wolverine hybrid. Now Ariel came forward and said "We are here to rescue your captives, let them go now!" Then the beast ran towards them and Ariel shape-shifted into the lioness of the Great Spirit. This monster rushed at Ariel with long fangs showing but she attacked, held it with her claws then ripping at its body she lunged her fangs into it and tore out its throat. As this was the strongest and thane leader of the wolverine pack that had been defeated and killed, no other dared to come forward and fight Ariel the victor lioness of the great spirit, and they all ran from the prison cave howling in surrender.

Chapter 30

A stra called out "Hello! Hello! Can you hear me?"
then a reply came back "Yes I can hear you, I
also heard the sounds of a terrible fight and the
cry's of our vicious captor in the pangs of death. Are you hurt?
This was followed by the sound of many whimpering Todd-
foxes who had been his only companions for many moons.
"No I am not injured, it was the angel Ariel the lioness of the
great-spirit that is the victor, she conquered your captor, and
now you are all free." "Oh! Praises to the great-spirit, and our
grateful thanks to the Arc Angel Ariel, where are you? It is so
dark in here and I have not seen the light since my capture."
Astra could see him he was sitting down leaning on a rock
surrounded by all the Todd-foxes. She went to him and took
his arm saying "Stand up and I will help you to walk, but first
you and these dear little creatures must be healed. As a healer
woman I will stand down as there is a superior healer with
me, this is the healing Arc Angel Raphael and he will heal

115

your eyes and do all healing that you all require." Raphael came forward and healed them all, and then they went out of the cave, giving thanks and praise to the great-spirit.

Now that they were in the light they could see each other for the first time. The Arc Angel Haniel stood behind them and blessed them with love peace and passion, and with that the law of spiritual attraction took over and they knew that they were soul mates. Michael the leader told them that it was time for them to return to earth, and that all the angels would accompany them and the Todd-foxes on the long journey home. When they were on their way home Astra asked if they could stop over in the constellation of her animal spirit protector Ursa Major the great bear. They consented and said that they would also like to pay their respects to Ursa. He was so happy to see them and thanked the Angels for taking time to visit him. They stayed with him for two moons and then resumed their journey. On the way Astra asked this very handsome Immortal what his name is. He just laughed and apologised for not introducing himself. "I am Todd Mac Adam and the thane protector of all these beautiful foxes that is why they are called Todd's and they will always live with me."

Before they entered the earth's gravitational pull the angels said farewell and told them that they could always call on them for help, if they needed it. They landed on the ice cold frozen earth just behind the forest near the Mac village and hastily made their way to Astra's house. Iris and the babies were there to welcome them, and there was a fire in the hearth. Hawk had kept it burning for Iris and the little ones. Cor knew that her twin had returned by the warm loving feeling she suddenly got. "Let us go and check if Astra is home, I have a feeling that she is near" Hawk agreed and the threesome went to visit. Iris started hissing and rattling to announce their arrival and the little ones did the same but went straight to their father, they loved to play with him.

Cor and Astra hugged each other and jumped up and down with glee, they did not like to be separated for long periods, now that they had found each other. Then Hawk came and gave Astra a hug and asked her to tell them about her experiences.

"Well news of all the events will have to wait for another day; I have something very exciting to tell you, and also to show you. I found, and with the help of the Arc Angel Ariel rescued my own Immortal man from being held captive by hybrid wolverines in the constellation of Vulpecular.

He was there for many moons with all the captive Todd-foxes that he protected. One night after a very exhausting journey he stopped to sleep for a while, and was taken captive by various species of carnivores. They were put into a cave that was guarded by the vicious wolverines. Come and meet the family she called" Then he came from another room and said "Hello I am Todd Mac Adam and I am originally from the constellation of Dorado in the Southern end of the universe, it is the home of the Dolphins many of them have been sent into the seas around Atlantis. These wonderful creatures help you find true love and are great friends of the Goddess Aphrodite."

Cor held her breath for a while, she did not know how many Immortals were created but what she did know was that two of them were right here in the Mac village. "Oh! please forgive me I am just surprised to see you and the tod-foxes, I thought that Astra had come back alone. I am Cor the thane leader and healer woman of the Mac clan village. You are all most welcome here. This is my Immortal man Hawk Mac Allan." Hawk stepped forward and shook hands with Todd and they smiled at each other. "It has been many ages since we last met said Hawk" "Yes you are right, I recall that it was when you fought Angus Mac Duff and sent his spirit back to Wathemera. Yes so very long ago replied Todd." Cor and Astra had turned a very pale shade of blue, each realising that inevitably these two would have to fight each other for the superior thane title. The only immortal being left on earth. Massassuga and Iris quickly slithered over to them and coiled around their companions, hissing in their ears. "Do not fret these two will not fight each other until there is no one left to defend the title presently held by James Mac Arthur. We can assure you both that it will not happen in your lifetime." The twins breathed a sigh of relief and brought a nice hot herb brew and a piece of honeycomb to eat, and they all chatted happily through the night.

Chapter 31

Time was not of an issue during the winter seasons as there was very little light that shone through the dark and heavy snow clouds. Everyone stuck to the rules that Cor had laid down, eat when you are hungry, drink when you are thirsty, sleep when you are tired, just do what comes naturally. Many women made hide tunics and boots, and others made fur coats and night covers for the beds.

The men made wooden articles for everyday use around the home and also wove basket nets to haul in the small fish during the summer months, they all kept themselves occupied. Astra and Todd were telling everyone all about the constellation of Vulpecular and of their experiences while they were there. Suddenly the frozen earth begun to shake and an unearthly high pitched screeching noise could be heard from a distance. The harder the earth shook the louder the noise got. "That can not be the wild ox it is not the season for them to roam around here, and there is no grass for them to graze" said Cor. "There is only one species of beast that is capable of this kind of behaviour" said Todd "It is one that the foxes and I have heard many times, do you recognise it Astra?" "Indeed I do it is the Mammoth is it not?" "You are right and if they run through the village then everything will be turned into rubble and everyone will be trampled to death. Come on Hawk we must side track them."

Cor and Astra had that blue look again, and their companions hissed and rattled and said "Do not fret precious angels, they are Immortals and will not be killed in the stampede. They will just attract the leader's attention and run away from the direction of the village, then the mammoths will follow them and your Immortal men will be heroes." Hawk and Todd came back inside and rushed to sit next to the hearth, and that dreadful noise was slowly fading into the distance, only to be followed by screeches and growls and roars and cries of pain and distress. Obviously this was what had caused the mammoths to stampede. Hawk and Todd went out again and saw that the sabre tooth was attacking the mohound-moloch hybrids that had been hunting the mammoths.

"This is a lucky break, look the striped cat is going to kill off every shape-shifting devil of Idiomia, and none will return to warn the others, so we can happily agree that there are about one hundred less now, yes! yes! yes! said Hawk." "Come let us go and tell our lassies the good news, yelled Todd" against the icy falling snow. They decided to roll down the brae and the snow caked up all around them turning them into laughing snow-balls that split open when they bumped into the wall of Astra's house. Iris hissed "Do they ever grow up?" and went back to sleep. Cor and Astra went and dusted the snow off of them before they came into the house. Todd told Astra that it is the sabre-tooth that are attacking the mohound-moloch hybrids who were hunting the mammoth.

They sat chatting about the times gone bye, and of the times yet to come, each giving his and her opinion of what is going to happen. They were so deep in thought and debate that they never noticed that both Mitzion and Blithe had come to pay a visit. Massassuga and Iris hissed and performed a side winding slither that indicated that they were honouring the presence of a spiritual Deity. This action caught their attention and they immediately apologised to them. Suddenly Ursa also put in an appearance, saying to Mitzion and Blythe, "Shall we get on with it please lassies as I have other urgent matters to attend to." Then he told Blithe to stand next to Cor and Hawk, and Mitzion to stand next to Astra and Todd, Massassuga and Iris each coiled around their life long companions and then Ursa announced that they had come to join these to couples in wedlock, as they were ordered to do so by Wathemera. "Do you promise to cherish each other as long as you live and remain faithful to each other until death separates your bodies and souls from your spirits?

"Yes we do replied Hawk and Cor, followed by the same reply from Todd and Astra. Then there were hisses and rattles from the coiled ones giving their approval and consent." Then be blest by the Great Spirit and carry out his plan for your lives together," said Ursa, Blythe and Mitzion rendered the wedlock chant for physical and spiritual union. Now Ursa announced that Cor Mac Maure would now be known as Cor Mac Allan, and Astra Mac Maure would now be known as Astra Mac Adam. "You are eternal twin flames each with the other as announced in the sight of the Great Spirit Wathemera." Now there were six hissing, rattling, side winding young witnesses that came forward and three joined their Mother and three joined their Father eyes wide and sparkling with joy.

The two Goddesses performed the wedding feast cantrip and magically there was a banquet set before them all. Everyone ate and drank and danced well into the wee hours, and then Ursa and the Goddesses returned to their own constellations waving farewell. However there was a mess left in the house after the festivities but Cor and Astra chanted the cantrip for cleanliness and tidiness and magically the mess disappeared before their eyes and everything returned to normal again.

The couples hugged and congratulated each other, and Hawk and Todd announced that they were now brothers and would remain loyal to each other for the duration of their wedded life to the twins.

Chapter 32

Cor Hawk and Massassuga said that they were going home now, and covered their heads with a fur.

As the icy snow was lashing in every direction they made a dash for the comfort of their home which was not very far from Astra and Todd's home. Once inside Massassuga just fell off Cor and on to the fur next to the hearth as he had almost frozen in that position around Cor when the lashing ice crystals cut into his scales. He hissed and sighed but could not rattle as that part of him was almost frozen solid. They had a hot herb drink and then went to bed and with their bodies close and intertwined for warmth among other things they went off to dreamland covered by thick fur pelts.

In Astra and Todd's house in front of the hearth with a comforting hot herb brew they discussed all the unexpected events of the day. Iris was hissing and never seemed to stop but she was getting a sore throat from all the hissing and it became softer and quieter but none the less never stopped. It was annoying Todd as he was not used to her and her way of giving a hint. When he looked over at her she was standing up on her tail and looked cross eyed at him, but he never understood what she was up to. He went over to her fur covered corner and bending over her he said, "If you do not stop now I will throw you outside and let you freeze." "Oh! right, and if you don't take her to bed now she will throw you outside and let you freeze numbskull, I have been trying to hint to you all night.

I sure hope that, that is the only part of you that is numb, hiss, hiss, Immortal indeed, man huh!!?" "Immortal, caring, loving, tender, gentle, protecting, kind man not a snatch and grab opportunist."

"Did you think that I would say, 'Into bed with you and wait until I'm through bam, bam, thank you mam now go and bring me some brew'? honestly Iris, shut those beady eyes and go to sleep alone, ha, ha, ha" she very coyly said "I am sorry" so he bent over a little more and kissed her on the head, "Friends now all is forgiven sleep tight, that is with both eyes Iris" in answer she stuck her tongue out at him and smiled. Now just to prove to her who is the thane leader in this house he went and joined Astra on the fur at the hearth and they both enjoyed another hot herb brew.

After which Todd moved closer to Astra and taking her in his arms he kissed her tenderly and said "Do you think that it is bed time yet my angel"? "I thought that you would never suggest it, I thought that just maybe Immortal men never slept" she teased smiling at him and with a gleam in her eyes jumped up and taking him by the hand said "Come I want to see what Immortal men are made of" and they went off into the bed room with arms around each other. Iris sighed and said "At last, thank you Wathemera, hee, hee, now I will sleep with one eye open."

They undressed and as was the custom in those days went to bed naked. As Astra was about to get into the bed Todd took her around the waist and said "I thought that you wanted to see what Immortal men are made of my dearest, turn around and have a look" "Wow what is this?" she asked taking his long thick erect appendage in her hand. "It resembles Iris when she stands up on her tail but why has it only got one eye?" Todd burst out laughing "Oh you precious innocent little one, it is not a snake, it is the reproductive organ of the male, we have all got one, even those that are not Immortal. It is with this one eyed appendage that we procreate as the Great Spirit intended us to"

Now holding it in both her hands she said "Well then get on with it procreate and let me see, no! wait a little, look it's eye is starting to cry there is a tear coming out of it, maybe it dose not want too do the procreation thing, I will just kiss it on it's head." As she bent forward to kiss this dear sad appendage Todd picked her up and put her on the bed, then laying on his back he said "Go on little darling now you can kiss it all you want" Astra sat astride him and bent over to kiss him on the mouth but as she did so this beautiful sad appendage suddenly jerked and slipped into her birth canal, and then he rolled her over onto her back and it started to move, slowly and that hurt and she yelled "AW, that is sore, stop it" but he just said "it wont be sore any more it always is the first time" He eased it into her with slow movements and then she smiled and said "It is nice now do not stop," then the movements became very rapid and Astra felt the most wonderful sensation and a burst of warm fluid filled that cavity that had always felt so empty, and both these fantastic sensations happened at the same time as Todd shuddered and stopped moving.

He started kissing her all over her body and she said between gasps of pure joy, "Wow was that called procreation?" "Well it is the loving act of procreation but a baby only forms when the Great Spirit decides that the time is right." "So do we have to keep doing that delightful act until Warthemera decides that the time is right" "Yes we do and we can do it as often as we want too"

"Well all I can say is that Wathemera sure knows what he is doing, it is no wonder that they call him the Great Spirit, come on lets do it again, and again, and again" she even sang those 'again' words with a smile and with a joyous tone." "Just as well that I am an Immortal other wise you would kill me doing the loving act, but what a pleasure it would be to die like that. My fear is that it will exhaust you so much that you would die before the Great Spirit decides the time is right for our baby to be born." "Not a problem have you forgotten that I am the twin of Cor and therefore have the same abilities as she has? I too am a Sharminn healer woman and share the 'thane position' as she dose. So you see when ever I think that I am going to die, I will just heal myself, and then we can do it again, and again, and again." They both laughed until their stomachs hurt and then cuddling and kissing they intertwined their legs and finally went to sleep.

All this joy made Iris long for the warmth of Massassuga, so when the babies were asleep she slithered out and went and coiled up with him, and that is where Cor and Hawk found them fast asleep with big smiles on their faces, in the morning.

Chapter 33

Ahealer woman came to call Cor as there was another birthing problem, she called out that she would follow her, but she must go and call Astra to join them as she sensed that this was double trouble again, and she wanted her twin to assist her. Together they followed the woman to a house very near the sea. Cor could not understand why this woman was pregnant as her husband had frozen to death two winters ago while on look out duty. She confided her worry to Astra that this just might be another mohound-molock hybrid Idiomian devil that had got hold of her. When they got there the twins both recognized that she was a Dragonfae being one of their own kind.

She was in agony and the baby was halfway out of her birth canal, but what they could see was the tail of a fish, then they both knew that the baby had more Mer-being cellular matrix and therefore would have a Mer body with all the traits as well. Then Astra said we will have to go into her and pull this one back the shoulders are too wide to pass through the birthing canal. Then they chanted the birthing chant and both went into her with their hands splitting her stomach open. The sight that met their eyes gave them both the chills, over and above the cold weather. These were twins and they were joined at the head. They took the one and lifted it out and up and gently pulled the other one back until they were both free.

Cor attended to the mother and healed her large gaping wound, while Astra did a separation chant and freed the babies from what would have been a life of total disfigurement and constant frustration, then she healed their head wounds. "What beautiful little Mer beings they are said Astra but as you know, you will have to spend more time in the water with them than out of it.!" "May I ask you how you got pregnant seeing that you have no husband?" asked Cor. "Yes I will tell you.

I was very lonely when he died and I often went and sat on the rocks by the sea and cried, I used to look out into the distance and ask the Great Spirit to send me someone to love again. After some moons had come and gone, one day a handsome Mer-man came and we chatted about so many things. He came every day and we fell in love and mated in the water. We did this very often as we enjoyed the pleasure derived from this act of intimate love. One day I told him that I was not feeling very well and that there was something moving around inside of me. He was filled with joy and hugged and kissed me, and then he told me that we are going to be parents, because the movement inside of me was our very own baby. I can just imagine how pleased he will be when I tell him that we have twins. Thank you both so much for helping me and the little ones, may the Great Spirit bless you both abundantly.

On the way home Astra said "Cor I wonder which of our cellular matrix will be the most prominent do you think that the Dragonfae cellular matrix will be stronger than the Immortal cellular matrix?"

"Yes, I do not think that we need to be concerned about that, the Dragonfae will be stronger because the great spirit only created a certain number of Immortals, and there will only be one left when his Devine timing takes his entire creation of spirit beings back to the source of it's genesis".

"Then do you think that our children will look like us, or do you think that one of our cellular matrix hybrids will be stronger and we might even have a little Dragon, or a little Mer being, or a little Angel, or a little fae. All these matrixes are blends of our Dragonfae being?" "Astra I do not care which of them is the stronger cellular matrix just as long as it is small when it is born, and grows big and strong and becomes a wise and beautiful adult. I would hate to have to suffer like some of the unfortunate woman that I have helped with the birthing process. Actually if the love making was not so exciting and enjoyable, I would never do it just to be on the safe side. Well here is your house and there is mine, and we both have a real flesh and blood handsome powerful man waiting inside to welcome us home and warm us up. Let us go in and tease them into a frenzy of lovemaking, oooooooooow I can't wait for this void to be filled again, can you? Bye for now"

With great expectations they went into their homes, only to find that their Immortal men were not there. However their lifelong companions informed them that the news of another Immortal having slain the then champion James Mac Arthur, had got to them both and the fact that he was inviting someone to challenge him got them interested to take advantage of the invitation. Cor and Astra were very upset as they knew that this could end the life of one of their beloved husbands. "Who is the champion thane Immortal that has sent the invitation to challenge him for the title?" asked Cor.

Iris answered "It is the feared Mick Mac Fadden. He is known as the Red teind bearded Immortal standing at eight Rigel in height, and having a trone-weight more than that of two cuddy-donkeys, the one that all the Immortals have feared since his time began. He comes from the northern constellation of Hercules and has been presently transmuted to our planet mother earth." "Where is this contest to take place?" Asked Astra. "It was reported that it is to take place on the Nevis of Ben Macdhui, the highest and most dangerous of all the Bens." replied Iris. "Cor we must go and watch this battle, come let us go now!" "No we must not leave the village without a thane-leader, anything can happen and there will be no one with authority and no one with superior sharminn ability. You know very well that there are all types of beasts and hybrids of every kind migrating from all over. No! one of us will have to stay, and seeing that you have just returned from a Galactic travel, I think it is only fair that I should go." Astra was downhearted but agreed that Cor was right so she decided to remain in the village.

Chapter 34

Cor left with Massassuga who was determined that he would sneak up on this Giant of a man and deliver an extra venomous bite to his ankle, if he was getting the better of either Hawk or Tod. Cor told him that it would be unethical and unfair, also that the Great Spirit would be vexed as that was not the reason why he created immortals. He argued that the Giant would not die from the venom he might just be weakened and then his competitor would stand an even chance. Cor told him that all Immortals have an even chance no matter what their size is. He sulked and refused to talk to her anymore. When they arrived in the area they had to cross the river Ythan that was frozen just as everything else was, but the ice had a different texture, and on two occasions Cor slipped and fell, only to get hisses from Massassuga. Now they had to climb the Ben to the Nevis where there was a section of level Ice, the going up was dangerous as there were icy crags and many deep gorges.

When they got there they saw four other Immortals but Hawk and Tod were nowhere to be seen.

Cor's heart almost stopped, and she uttered softly, "they must have been defeated already . . ." With tears streaming down her checks she sat down to have a rest and then Massassuga said "I smell no blood you are not concentrating, what is wrong with you? you should have sensed that there has been no death here yet. Pull yourself together now Cor if you want to watch, otherwise let us go back home." No matter how hard she tried she could not stop and then the nerves in her stomach started to cramp and she retched, and cried and retched again and kept this up for a while. Now Massassauga got worried and did not know what to do, he was at his wits end. He started to slither around hissing and rattling and slipping and sliding and then he fell down a slight narrow gorge, and got the shock of his life, now he was gasping for air as he had hurt himself and could see a gash in his side. He had to get back to Cor she was sick and alone and that was his main objective, "I must hurry, got to get there, got to find her," so he painfully carried on going up and slipping down again, and this was repeated over and over again. Eventually he found her and now she was laughing almost hysterically. "Oh! dear she has gone into shock" he muttered.

Slowly he dragged his sore almost frozen body up on to her lap and then he coiled himself all around her trying to keep the falling icy snow off her and maybe warm her up a little.

"I am so happy that you are back, I would never have fitted in there" she said and kissed him right between the eyes.

"No, but the Cor that I know and love would have levitated me out of there, what is wrong with you anyway? You have got me very worried now." "I know what is wrong with me, when you fell down the gorge, I jumped up to help you and that is when I felt it." "The cramp again was it very bad?" "No my dearest companion, not a cramp, it is a baby moving inside of me! Hawk and I are going to have a little one," Massassuga's eyes squinted then he fainted and fell down around Cor's feet. Looking down at him she saw the gaping wound that was half the length of his body, and knew how much pain he must have been in and how he had struggled to get back to her. Cor healed him and tucked him under her fur to warm his almost frozen body.

A voice echoed through the surrounding Ben's "Top o' the morning to ye all, as an eternal slumber will follow those that challenge me, get ready to meet the great spirit in his dimension,

Well, well, what have we here? Four confidant Immortals, well come hither laddy's who is the first of ye? I love to see heads roll that is why I chose the highest Ben, come on now who is first, step forward" Logan Mac Elder stepped forward he was almost a match in size and weight. Then Cor saw Hawk and Tod approaching and ran to them, begging them not to challenge any of the contestants. She said Immortality is almost for eternity and they still have many years and there are many Immortals. She convinced them not to challenge any Immortal during her and her twin's lifetime, and their lives together as man and wife. She asked them to promise that they would only watch. They both smiled and promised that they had only come to watch and not take part in any contest at all.

Logan Mac Elder drew his skean-sword and so did Mick Mac Fadden, they touched the tips saying in unison "May the best man win" then they started circling each other and making a jab at the body every now and then. Mick's long tangled red teind-hair flew around his head and the beard flew up into his eyes, masking his vision every time that he turned very fast and doubled back on his own direction, trying to confuse Logan. All the on lookers could see that they were moving closer to the edge of the Ben while clashing their skean-swords and yelling outrageous abuse at each other, then just as Mick was about to strike at Logan's head there was a thunderous noise and the ice broke under his great trone weight and he fell feet first down into the gorge below but as he was falling Logan leaned forward and struck, so it was the loud mouthed Mick Mac Fadden's head that rolled down the side of the Ben. Now Logan called out any challengers for me but no one went forward and it was then concluded that Logan was the reigning champion Immortal for the time being. They decided that the next challenge would be after the winter ice season was over as it was to precarious duelling on the slippery icy surfaces.

Cor breathed a sigh of relief and Hawk put his arm around her and they all started on their homeward journey. Meanwhile back at the village Astra was troubled by a striped sabre tooth that had discovered the storage cave entrance, and was raiding it. She told Iris that they would have to spend the night in the cave in order to trap and destroy the thief. Iris adjusted her colouring to the exact colour of the dried meat and Astra transformed her into looking just like an appetising large piece. She lay on top of the pile and waited, while Astra shape-shifted into another sabre tooth, and crouched in the corner behind the entrance. When the moon was high in the sky they heard grunting and snarling and then it appeared in the cave and went straight to the meat storage pile. It was dark in the cave and it took some slices in its mouth among which was Iris. As it turned around to leave with a mouthful to go and eat in its own den, Iris delivered a venomous bite to the inside of its mouth. The big striped malkin-cat tossed all the meat at the wall with tremendous power and started to run out of the cave but the poison that Iris had injected started to paralyse it and it tried to drag its self away from the cave. Astra shape-shifted back into her own form and did a petrifying cantrip-spell on the sabre-toothed transforming it into solid rock. She levitated it and placed it at the entrance to the cave. Then she turned to get Iris who was stunned by the contact with the rock face wall and revived her dear life companion thanking her for her help.

Chapter 35

A woman from the constellation of Draco was giving birth to her first baby and having difficulty,

When she realised that she needed assistance she sent her husband to ask Astra to come and help her. This was a very painful birth as her birthing canal tore as the little one pushed its own way out with very powerful actions. Astra said "Well what do you know, look you have given birth to our first baby dragon and she is so very beautiful" then she healed the mother's wound and brought the baby to her. She was the image of her Father and just a little bit like her mother who was a hybrid.

They were very grateful and told Astra that the village people could call on them at any time if they could help with anything. She went home with Iris draped over her shoulder, and they were both grateful for the warmth of the hearth. The babies were at the naughty stage and had got up to all sorts of mischief. They had been in the honey vat and were all gooey. Then they rolled on Astra's bed cover fur and the fine hairs were sticking to them. With six sticky babies rolling all over to try and get not only the hairs and honey off of themselves but the whole fur cover because it had stuck to all of them and they were tied up in knots, hissing their heads off and getting nowhere.

They got a forked tongue lashing from Iris, and Astra was so vexed that she pulled them off one at a time. Hissing and rattling they each had to have a cantrip-spell performed on them by Astra to dissolve and remove all the mess off of them. Iris refused to give them their usual dinner of a small rodent; she sent them to bed without food. "You just wait until your father comes home he will teach you all a lesson, yes he will, now go to sleep all of you!" Astra said that her back and her head hurt, so Iris slithered over to the herb rub for pain, and dipped herself in it and then side winded over her back again, and again, and again until she went to sleep then she rubbed a little on her forehead with her lower jaw, and hissed "sleep well my angel." In the morning all the babies were missing and Iris was panicking, she went and woke Astra with the news and together they searched everywhere but in vain. Iris started to slither behind every item in the house and made an amazing discovery. Behind the honey vat was a small heap of sand with a hole in the middle, this she knew was either the home of a mole or a vole or another type of reptile that lived underground. She hissed her detection excitedly out to Astra and went down the hole. Sure enough all the babies were there and fast asleep, their stomachs distended, which indicated that they had over eaten. Very relieved Iris went back up and had a rest on her fur bed.

Cor Hawk, Tod and Massassuga were almost home when another blizzard struck and the restless north wind caused the icy snow to crystallise and cut into everything that had not iced up completely. The four would have frozen to death if it were not for the fact that two were immortals and Cor was able to perform any miracle with her sharmannic abilities. She did the chant for all their auras to radiate enough heat to cover and protect them from the cold and also from frostbite.

The sharp ice crystals that would have hit them started to melt and fall when they struck their warm auras. Feeling the chill in the air but not at all harmed, they finally reached home. Astra and Iris were excited and grateful to Wathemera for the safe return of all their loved ones. Astra prepared a warm herb drink and some food for the cold and weary travellers. They all sat around the hearth and exchanged the various events that they had all withstood. Six playful babies came up from their underground retreat hissing "Look father is home", and they made straight for him and started to play all over his aching body. He just smiled and went cross eyed in disapproval of their antics but said "Hello my dearest little ones, I am so glad to see you but can we play a little later on, I am exhausted right now, and I want to sleep a little." So they left him and went and tackled their mother, knowing that she got impatient with them after a while, and would send them off in another direction. Never mind there was plenty to explore, and maybe they would find something nice to eat again. With twinkling eyes they went off in different directions to investigate.

Cor spoke and said that she had information that was known only to her and Massassuga on the planet earth. "I want to tell you all that I have discovered that Hawk and I are going to be parents"

Hawk jumped up and took her in his arms and asked "Why did you not tell me Cor?" "Well I only discovered it myself up on the Ben Machudi. I was not feeling well and then I started to retch violently quite a few times. Then when Massassuga fell down the gorge, I jumped up to go and get him and that was the first time that I had felt something moving inside of me. That is when I knew that a little one is on the way." "I am so happy my darling and now you must be careful what you do." "Yes you must rest more often now Cor, and let Astra do the more difficult things" said Tod.

She said that she was in good health and had never felt stronger in her life, but promised that she would leave the more difficult things for her twin to do. Then to celebrate they each had a wee drab o' mead.

Chapter 36

Now all the creatures that the Great Spirit Wathemera had created in the constellations were very restless and causing trouble among themselves. Contests and challenges were becoming a commonplace event and they usually lasted all day. Many beasts in every constellation were dying from the wounds that they had received. Wathemera looked down from his abode at the Zenith of the universe, and decided to release a few beasts from every constellation. Then he called upon all the Dragons from the constellation of Draco to go down before he transmuted the others, and use their fire flames to melt the ice. He stopped the snow and in place of it he sent the rain and all the seeds sprouted in the soil that had been frozen. All the food sources that were required for the nutrition of the life forms that he had created grew abundantly, and the trees and shrubs were beautiful and green again.

Cor sent the first watch out now as she knew that there would be many dangers around. The Goddesses Blithe and Mitzion had come to her and told her of the intentions of Wathemera to send new life forms down on to the earth as their new home. They said that there were many that were very dangerous and also powerful. She was advised to tell everyone in the Mac village to be constantly on the look out for anything unusual and report it to her and Astra immediately. They also said that Wathemera was going to give Cor and Astra much more power than they had before. He said that they would have more visits from their ben-side grandmother and all the ancestors that had gone to the spirit world, as they would need assistance with the great influx of various creatures. She was advised to put up watch towers made from the large trees, with platforms for them to stand on. They would have to be high up in order to see into the distance, and these watch towers must be placed all around the now extended village. Cor ordered that this be done as fast as possible. She sent the initiates out to look for more large horns of plenty uses, as each man on the watch would need one for warning purposes.

That night there was a great shaking of the earth and it split apart down the far west side, and then a tremendous explosion almost deafened everyone as the Ben Machudi burst at the top and spewed red molten lava high into the atmosphere. It was raining fire all over the Ben and surrounding areas.

There was a curve in the low lying troussachs, and a large slant in the earth that caused the lava flow to run into the recently made gorge, and thus avoid the village on the way to the sea. Although the Mac village was facing the east the humungous lava flow had to either cover it or bypass it via the gorge In the morning Cor asked Astra to tell the watch to sound the gathering call on the horn of plenty uses. She did that and then told the villagers to come with her up to the henge of stone to give praise and thanks to the Great Spirit for sparing their lives. While she was up there she had a feeling that Cor needed her because she was nowhere to be seen. She told Hawk and Tod that she was going to Cor because she thought that the baby was about to come into the world.

Hawk was not going to miss the birth of his baby, and neither were Tod and Iris. So they all went as quickly as was possible. On the way down they were met by an anxious Massassuga who was on his way up to call Astra. He was almost out of breath and just said "hurry the baby is coming and Cor is in so much pain, hurry, hurry!" Hawk picked him up and draped him over his shoulder because he thought that the exhausted life companion of his beloved wife was about to pass out."

When they arrived at the house Cor was walking around and around in circles, clutching her abdomen, she was very hot and the sweat was running down her face and body. "Oh! I am so relieved to see you Astra I thought that I would have to give birth all alone, Aww, ooou, I am so sore". Astra was pleased to see that the pains were still far apart, that gave her time to do the chant for safe birthing and then no harm would come to Cor or the baby. That having been done, she told Cor to lie down so that she could examine her. To

Astra's surprise she could feel that the baby was almost in the birth canal, but what was that other movement a little higher up? "I think that there is more than one baby in there Cor, you must prepare yourself for a longer labour" Now the pain was excruciating and she knew that she had to squat, after about ten minutes Astra caught the baby, and Cor lay down to rest." What is my baby"? she asked. "It is the most beautiful Dragonfae girl" she said, and wanted to give her to Cor but the next pain came and the whole thing started all over again, so she gave the baby to Hawk to hold. Massassuga was slithering around hissing and rattling

"Just look at him anyone would think that he was the father, he can not be still for a moment." Said Todd.

Then there was another cry and Astra told Cor that there was another baby still waiting to come.

"This is another beautiful baby girl, and also Dragonfae, you must get ready for the third one now"

She gave the second one to Tod to hold, he was very happy to do so. Now she told them that a third one was on the way. Hawk was excited about having sired triplets, but very worried about Cor. Quite sometime later Astra came out holding another baby, and said "This is the last one Hawk and it is your son, what a handsome strong lad he is, here take him, I have to attend to Cor now." Massassuga was sulking and then Hawk gave him permission to get up and cuddle the babies, so Tod put the other little girl in the middle of the two that were on Hawk's lap and he coiled himself around them all and smilingly he hissed "Congratulations Lord and Master but now I must go to our beloved Cor and congratulate her and soothe her as I always have through her life time."

"Hello my beloved Cor I am so relieved that the birthing is over now, congratulations on your three beautiful babies. These are nothing else but royal babies I hope that Hawk will allow me to suggest names for them even if he selects others" he hissed with a smile. "Here comes your Immortal Man and the babies now, so I will leave you alone and go to visit Iris and our brood, bye, bye," Hawk came into the room caring the babies and put them on the bed next to Cor. Then he leaned over and kissed her tenderly saying "Thank you my angel for bearing my beautiful babies, I love you so much but I have no words to express my feelings and I can not even hold you in my arms for sometime yet" "I know just what you mean Hawk so I will keep those special thoughts in my mind not just for now but for always, they are beautiful babies, only your babies could look so beautiful. I am a very blessed mother to have our babies sired by such a handsome strong Immortal my love"

"Have you thought about names for them yet daddy?" "No my angel as you know I was expecting only one and I did not know what it would be, so now we will have to make a list and choose from it together, will that be in order?" "Yes it will be in order but can we also take names that Massassuga has for them into consideration please?" "Sure we can, I will call him in and then we can decide." Hawk went to call Massassuga from Iris's house and he went slithering ahead of Hawk and got up on the bed with her and the new born little ones smiling and softly hissing in contentment.

"Well now life long companion of my beloved Cor, let us hear what you have to say." said Hawk.

"I would like to put a question to you both before I tell you which names Iris and I have chosen for your consideration. We want to give the babies each a gift of a life long companion from our brood, if you are both willing to accept the gifts". "Oh! how wonderful they said simultaneously."

Chapter 37

"Well now here goes! The girls: Dautie-meaning darling, Leal-meaning faithful, and The Lad: Bruce—meaning King." Hawk and Cor looked at each other in amazement and both nodded their approval, as if having been dumbstruck. "This is too good to be true said Hawk, we could not have found better names ourselves, so let it be written and so let it be said." Then Iris came in with the little ones all smiling and hissing. They put Cor's babies down on the ground to see which little companion would go to which baby, and the ones that chose a life companion would be the ones to stay with the child for ever. Massassuga and Iris were hybrids from their past ancestors and so their babies were also hybrids. It was quite clear that some had a stronger cellular matrix than others and the various ones showed up in their off spring. They were slithering around the babies sniffing each one, in order to make up their minds which one they wanted to commit their life time to. Krait was the first one to choose, she was black with the red stripe right down the centre of her back that came from her hybrid matrix and she chose to be the life companion of Dautie, Krait lay over the baby's stomach and went to sleep. Then Cerastas who was a horned viper hybrid having the colours of brown with bright yellow patches diagonally all over her body went and lay over Leal's stomach and fell asleep. Now it was Bruce the King's turn and they never had so long to wait for his companion to choose him. It was the King Cobra hybrid with a grey body and patches of red and yellow over his entire body that went and lay over Bruce's stomach and his name was Hamadryad.

Iris went home to Astra who told her that they were going to travel in the cosmos again, only this time they were all going on an extensive time travel trip. It would include the past, present, and future. So they went to say good bye to the villagers and family, who were sad to see them go again.

Astra did the chant for cosmic time travel. And the violet flame of transmutation came down from out of the Universe and took Astra, Tod, Iris and the remaining little ones up and out of sight, on the most exciting venture of their lifetimes. They were on their way to Pegasus in the northern hemisphere, it is close to Andromeda and Pisces, Here they would find the most beautiful snow white creatures that were a hybrid of a winged horse and a Unicorn. They loved these creatures and asked the Great Spirit if he would please send them down to planet earth with them when they go back again. Wathemera agreed to send only a few with them. After staying there for a while they went on to visit the constellation of Serpens, so that Iris and her babies could mingle with the serpents and other reptiles that Wathemera had created there. All was agog and there was much hissing, spitting, slithering and side winding going on. Astra and Tod sat on a patch of grass on the side of a brae and watched as they all made their acquaintances. After some time there were three snakes of various hybrids that came and asked Iris' permission to take her little ones for mates, as it was time to introduce a new hybrid species in this constellation. She gave them her permission and they went off to mate and make a life of their own. Iris had tears in her eyes when she slithered up around Astra, who tried in vain to comfort her. Now it was time to leave this constellation and continue on their long journey, with a few new species that wanted to go to the earth with the Great Spirits permission.

As the years went by Dautie, Leal, and Bruce grew into wonderful specimens of their hybrid ancestors, and so did their life long companions. Bruce was showing signs of his Immortal cellular matrix taking a form towards his father's side. His features were very much like a hybrid of the Dragonfae, but he had the muscular shape, height and the mighty strength of his father.

Yes he had become even more powerful than his immortal father Hawk, because he could also shape-shift into anything like his Dragonfae mother Cor, so he had shape-shifting, healing and Immortality in his cellular matrix which would be passed on to further generations.

Dautie and Leal were Dragonfae with Cor's curvaceous body and beautiful blue eyes and good looks, but had inherited their fathers mighty strength too but not his Immortality.

Dautie had more of the Mer being matrix showing in her appearance as she had the Lemurian Mer being beautiful red hair and fair skin. Leal had more of the angelic cellular matrix showing in her appearance as she had developed the wings of an angel, and Devine wisdom.

Krait and Cerastes grew to the same length as Iris, but they were much broader in girth and far more venomous. They are as loyal and protective to Dautie and Leal as Iris is to Astra. Hamadryad was similar to Massassauga in nature but much different in appearance. He was as long and strong as his father 'that was the hybrid of the Boa constrictor' but his other quality was that of the King Cobra, so he was the most powerful and venomous reptile on the planet. Hamadryad is just as loyal and protective to Bruce as Massassauga is to Cor.

Chapter 38

The Blasties who had remained in obedience to the great spirit, and the Kelpies came to visit one fine summer day, and told Cor that they had come across many weird and dangerous hybrid-being species that they had not seen before. Cor explained that the Great Spirit had sent Blyth and Mitzion to inform her that he had transmuted many creatures that he had created in the constellations down to earth. It was now his Devine timing for them to migrate and populate the entire planet with various hybrids of their own created kind. "So you see my precious little friends that is why you have encountered all these beings, and you are likely to see more and more of them as they are now mating and bringing forth an evaloution of new species here on our planet mother Gaia. They also told me that there would be a creation transmuted down here that would eventually be known as human, so we anxiously await their arrival. Should you ever see any please let me know?" They promised that they would and the Blasties left again on their nomadic roaming as usual while the Kelpies returned to their respective Burns, Rindles, and Lochs.

That night Ursa appeared and told Cor that there was going to be a tremendous conflict in the firmament. Super beings that wanted to rein supreme in the universe started the war. It was a war amongst the most intelligent beings ever created. None of the beings in any constellation were going to just accept this outrageous claim to fame and they all joined in a battle that went on for decades.

Down on earth if one looked up into the firmament on dark nights, one could see flashes of strange lights and thunderous noises could be heard. During the day one could only hear the noises from above. Hawk and Cor and their children feared that the battle might just also be transmuted to earth if the Great Spirit deemed it necessary. However that was not to be, but Wathemera had decided to send great earth quakes that split mother Gaia into separate sections, and he called them continents. Then he allowed the huge volcanic eruptions to explode on the earth, this happened on most of the continents and formed the trossachs and the Bens all over. Some sections that had split from the main body of mother Gaia had not quite separated in their entirety but were partly joined to the main continent. This made a way to cross from one part of the earth body to the other. Cor was thankful for that because of the Blasties nomadic lifestyle she would have been very upset if Wathemera had not left those cross over points and they were stuck in some unliveable part of the continents.

There were some very humanoid looking beings that had been transmuted via the violet flame. And they had been set down on the various continents. Ursa had reported that they were from Sirius B and were known as the Arkadians, then there were those from the star system of Arcturus located in the Bootes constellation, the Pleiadians were from the seven star system named the Pleiades, the Venusians are from the extremely hot planet of Venus. This planet is used as an intergalactic stop over for space travellers on their very long journeys between the constellations and planets, and always a place to have a most welcomed and well earned rest.

The Arcturians are a fifth dimensional civilization that use a kaleidoscopic energy force, thereby creating a constantly changing pattern of sequence while spinning with mother Gaia as she rotates on her own axis. These beings are geometric in form and create holographic imagery by which they communicate. Cor and Astra had learned this form of communication when on one of their intergalactic travels. They spent quite some time in the star system of Arcturus, with the Arch Angel Raziel who is the keeper of the universal secrets and is also a master in geometric formation and its style of communication. Cor having been blest with Devine wisdom knew that there were various dimensions that could be attained through open portals. She also knew that there would be a timeious shift in cosmic consciousness within Devine order. Presently there was one of those shifts taking place, and that is why the Great Spirit had ordered the transmutation of these compassionate and wise intergalactic beings to inhabit the earth, and mix their cellular matrixes with those of the Dragonfae, and the other celestial and territorial beings who already dwelt on the earth planet.

Chapter 39

Now the Great Spirit pondered over all his creations that he had transmuted to the earth planet, and decided that it was time to send some Gods down. He also decided to send Astra, Tod, and Iris back to their home in the Mac village of Caledonia, along with the beautiful white hybrid of the Unicorn and the winged horse Pegasus, as he had promised. The first rays of the sun peeped over the Ben near the Mac village, this Ben had not yet been given a name and as Massassuga slithered sleepily out of the house and with a longing in his heart for his beloved Iris he hissed and yawned and said "Good morning Mac Ben." He startled himself at having made the very first sound of the day, and then realising what he had just said he stood straight up on his tail, and smiled. He prided himself at having just given a name to a part of mother Gaia. Unbeknown to him Cor and Hawk were watching him and heard what he had just said, so they rendered an applause that echoed every where within a distance that far outreached the Forrest and the Bens beyond the Mac village. Little did they know that Massassauga had spent half the night with his head in the vat of mead commiserating with himself over the absence of Iris.

As night turned into day there was a slow soft rumbling sound that got louder and louder until it reached the Mac village and then there was an explosion of starlight. Thousands of little stars were lining a pathway that came from out of the universe all the way down to the earth. They stopped just behind the Forrest, and then there was the most beautiful sound of celestial singing. The entire population of the village ran into the Forrest to see what this event was all about. They were stunned into silence at what they saw. Astra with Iris, and then Todd next to them came riding on the most beautiful creatures they had ever seen. They were surrounded by little twinkling stars in the form of a ring around them and the creatures danced in tune to the celestial music. Massassauga thought that he was either inebriated, dreaming or had passed from this worldly life when he saw the spectacular entrance of the returning travellers, and yes! that was Iris with them, she had come back to him. It was all to much for him to comprehend and so he fainted. Behind them came a huge variety of creatures that Wathemera had promised to send along with Astra, Tod and Iris. They all mingled and introduced themselves to each other, then proceeded to go to the henge of stone to give praise and thanks to the great spirit for all the blessings that they had received. After that had been done Cor and Hawk, Astra and Tod, Massassauga and Iris got the villagers together and arranged the best celebration party that Caledonia had ever hosted.

On the following night the celestial trumpets sounded and the same stairway was visible but only in a more glorious array than the last one.

The Gods and Goddesses and many light beings including the delightful elementals came forward in an awesome descending parade, happy to join the resident beings of land, sea, and sky. However they stated that they would make their esteemed positions known and also demand that their rules would be adhered to and their commands obeyed. After this statement was made there was a thundering noise made by the night mares of the ben-side ancestor riders in the sky. They were screeching, and wailing and threatened to war against the Gods unless they retracted the statements that they had just made. They would not allow the Thane Sharminn and the Immortals to be degraded and dethroned by these new Gods and Goddesses under any circumstances.

Now Cor, Hawk, Astra and Tod knew their own strength as well as the powers of their ben-side ancestors, but they were reluctant to wager a bet on the strength and power of the Gods and Goddesses against them should a war be declared. The villagers all went to bed with much trepidation in their thoughts as they have never had anything to do with the Gods, and never knew any of them at all with the exception of Blythe and Mitzion.

Chapter 40

Massassauga and Iris however had no doubts, that the Gods although powerful would not stand a chance, as they were not immortal. "These Gods are vulnerable Iris, they can die and with you and I as unseen opponents, and with our triple potent venom the odds are against the Gods. Just one accurate strike will be fatal, and an ankle is about the right height for a slithering position jab. They will not be expecting an attack from the ground, now will they my love?" Iris agreed and so there were at least two that went to sleep without thoughts of trepidation that night. The next morning two wizards came to introduce themselves and offer their services to the villagers. They were well known amongst the Dragonfae and were loyal supporters of the sharminn since time immemorial, but the Mac clan had not yet met them. They were Merlin the first, and Gwydion the first and their magic would surpass any shape-shifting acts done by anyone except the sharminn. They were welcomed and performed many tricks to amuse the children, so needless to say they had a large following of loyal supporters.

Later a few Gods and Goddesses came and introduced themselves, but were very cautiously approached by the Mac clan.

"Hello to you all, I am Aine the Goddess of the Moon, and this is my sister Grian the solar Goddess and also the Queen of the Dragonfae" "I am Cerridwen the threefold Goddess and keeper of the triple cauldron, it is I who will defeat the three Carline witches and all their conspirators."

"I am Morrighan, the shape shifting Goddess of death and change, it is I who will totally annihilate the Mohound-devils and other evil beings and bring in a new way of living." "I am Oenghus the Celtic God of love and passion and it is I who find soul mates and bring them together . . ." "I am Llugh the Celtic sun god, and also the God of power and passion. I am the Celtic master shape-shifter and my favourite form is that of an Eagle"

Then Grian the Queen of the Dragonfae came forward and said "We have all come in love and peace and will assist you where ever we can. As Queen of the Dragonfae I wish to meet the Thane Sharminn Cor and her supreme twin Astra/. We share honoured cosmic positions, neither of us is superior to the other and we are therefore threefold etheric beings, and also shape shifters. Will you take me to them now please?" "Yes we will, please follow me said Mac Kay" and he took them to Cor and Astra.

"Hello Cor and Astra, I have had the honour of bringing guests to you, these are the Gods and Goddesses that have come to dwell here on the earth planet, and they request a meeting with you."

"Thank you Mac Kay" they said. "Good day to you all, we are very pleased to meet you. Would you mind following us to the Henge of stone where we have our meetings now, and that is also where we worship Wathemera" When they got to the Henge they all sat in a circle within the perimeter, and gave praise to the Great Spirit and asked for his blessing on this meeting and also for his Devine wisdom" Then Cor invited Grian the solar Goddess and their Dragonfae queen to speak.

Grain told them why they were here and then they all introduced themselves as they had done before to the villagers. "You are all most welcome but I would like to ask you a question please. We were under the impression that you have come to rule us and make us obey your commands, why do we have a different explanation from you?"

"The information that you received was from a shape-shifting Mohound that wanted you all to think that way, and therefore not accept us, but declare war between the Gods, the Immortals and the Dragonfae. Do not fear, Morrighan will destroy them and their home labyrinth Idiomia, then they will not trouble you anymore. Cerridwen will defeat the Carline witches and they will leave this planet. Together we will eradicate all the enemies of the past and a new generation of beings and beasts, will be here. We will still hunt and fish and plant and gather as before but without the present evil that is still around. My sister Aine the Moon Goddess will send the dark moon and all the enemies will not be able to detect us. We will all shape-shift into our spirit forms and be invisible to everyone and everything around. Llugh our master shape-shifter will transform into an eagle by day and an owl by night and from his place high in the sky will show us where to go if they start to hide."

"I Oenghus will bring soul mates together and there will be love, passion, and peace on the earth, that is the Devine will of the Great Spirit."

The Carlines and the Mohounds had a meeting and were discussing what cantrip-spells and shape shifting forms they were going to use in order to win the war that they were strategically arranging.

Suddenly there was darkness everywhere, and the Carlines looked up at the moon and yelled "Dark moon why have you lost your lustre,? What is the cause that your light withdraws, is it because you have deep secrets and are hiding them from us.?" Then they each tried their most powerful magic, to return the radiance to the moon but to no avail, and then they joined their evil magic together but in vain. The dark moon prevailed. Then Morrighan and Cerridwen moved into the labyrinthine dwellings, in ethereal incognito and obliterated the Carlines and the Mohounds and saturated the entire maze with the ethereal fluid-ichor and ethereal salt-ester. When their screeching stopped, there was silence on mother Gaia, and the dark moon withheld her splendour no more.

Chapter 41

True to his word Oenghus started out on a long journey to locate and unite soul mates that had not yet found each other. This was a very long and lonely time as he had to search the entire planet of Gaia, on land under the sea and in the astral realms, as these beings could be anywhere in Wathemera's creation. It had started in the Ordovician era about 510 million years ago. The Great Spirit specifically created beings that were capable of becoming hybrid ethnic clans until eventually they would migrate in cognized species and populate the entire planet.

Wathemera looked down on the planet Gaia and decided that it was time to send more God's and Goddess' from their domicile in the vast endless expanse. They were summoned to assemble in the constellation of Cepheus home of the monarchs.

When they all arrived Wathemera told them that they were going to be transmuted to the planet Gaia. He also said that they were going to be sent forth into the North, South, East and West in order to carry out their explicit capabilities, and that from henceforth on this would be their individual duty.

To name just a few of those selected for this era, there were in addition to the ones already sent:

ISIS, OSIRIS, HORUS, THOTH, SERAPIS-BEY, ATHENA, APOLLO, VISHNU, PARAVATI QUAN-YIN, and AVALOKITESVARA, these were very powerful Gods and Goddess'.

Many years had passed and Cor and Astra were very old, so the Great Spirit decided to recall them and all the Sharminn and Immortals, so that the God's and Goddess' could take their places and duties on mother Gaia. All those that were recalled went up to the henge of stone, there they worshipped Wathemera, and gave grateful thanks for the lives that they had on this earth and the wonderful unions they had, and all the experiences that they had shared. Cor and Astra requested that their life long loyal companions could accompany them and consent was granted. Massassauga and Iris slowly slithered around Cor and Astra giving thanks for the acknowledgement of their service and obedience to the Great Spirit. Hawk and Tod put their arms around Cor and Astra and together with all the other recalled beings went up into the cosmos via the violet flame of transmutation, once again to serve the Great Spirit however it pleased him.

They were allocated to a beautiful paradise as Ascended Masters because they had overcome all the limitations of hybrid being existence. Life on earth went on for many eons but the beings disobeyed the laws of Watherema, and he decided to punish them by total destruction of the world as they knew it, but he first recalled the Gods to their previous home. Then the sun and the moon were blackened and so were the stars, there was no light at all. Now the Great Spirit called the waters together and there was no land either. All life was destroyed.

However the Great Creator Spirit had a plan, and he decided to create once again on the planet Earth, but this time he would send the Gods down first. The earth would also be given a new dimension. And so the earth planet would be blessed with another period of a 5,125 year cycle of energy and human beings would be given their chance to obey the commandments of the Great Spirit, and answer to his call.

THE END

The Fugitive

Chapter 1

Ella January sat on a large rock a short distance from the shack she knew as home. She was sobbing as though her heart was about to break. She was desperate to get away from that place and all the abuse she had suffered. Her father had continually committed incest in his drunken state. He was always aggressive and beat her into unconsciousness if she did not do what he wanted. Often he drank so much mampoer that he never even went to work. The owner of the land on which he squatted told him that he would have to leave because of his intolerable behavior and the fights he caused amongst the other squatters. He was then given a month to find another piece of land on which to squat.

Her father then decided that he would not work again but would sell his daughter's services to all who would pay for them, and consequently made a good enough living to keep him comfortably supplied with mampoer and any other liquor that he could get his hands on.

As Ella sat there, with a faraway look in her eyes, she contemplated her escape. Just how would she manage to get enough distance between her and that place of her suffering and distress? She knew that when her father sobered up he would organize a search party to find her, Oh no! not because he loved her, but because she was his source of income and independence. Just how was she going to do it as she only had two sets of old worn out second-hand clothing and nothing else to her name. No jacket, no shoes and no money. In which direction should she go? She then remembered a prayer she had learned at the Mission Station, where she went whenever she could get away from her father.

"Angel of God my guardian dear to whom God's love commits me here, forever and this night be at my side, to light and lead, to guard and guide." She prayed these few words over and over and over again as she stared ahead. Then she heard the rumbling of thunder in the distance and saw the dark storm clouds gathering, and as it got closer the large rain drops started to fall on her from the sky. The lightening now snaked along with the oncoming storm and the rain drops turned into huge hailstones. She just sat there motionless and let them pelt her, after all, she had had more severe beatings from her father so what would a few more bruises matter. And that was when she heard the voice . . . . Go Ella, go now! Run into the storm, this is the chance that you have been waiting for!! . . . no one will follow you for any amount of money. Leave your other clothes and go!! I am your guardian Angel and I have heard your prayers and taken it to the Great Spirit, the Creator of the Universe and all in it, yes Ella to God himself. That is why this is such a very bad storm because God has sent it to save you from your persecution . . . . your divinely guided way to escape.

When she heard that she got up and started to run as fast as her legs could carry her. She ran blindly into the storm, through ditches and thorn trees, and the never ending sharp stones. On and on she ran getting encouragement from her little Angel who was at her side. Now as she ran she sang her prayer "Angel of God" and her Angel sang back to her, go Ella go, go Ella go, and on they went into the unknown. Ella never knew where she was going but she knew why.

The storm subsided and Ella was exhausted from her tremendous life and death rush for freedom. In the distance she saw a large bush and crawled under it for protection and a well deserved rest and immediately fell asleep. When she awoke it seemed as if she had been asleep forever. She thought "if only that was a nightmare that I had, but I know it was a real life experience of physical and emotional abuse."

She said her little Angel prayer again, and also thanked her for helping her through the most awful time in her life, thanked her also for helping her to escape, then she burst into tears and cried and screamed and thumped the ground to get rid of her lifelong frustration. In doing so she asked her little Angel to comfort her.

Then she heard a different voice, but it was a familiar one. She recognized it and knew that what it said seemed just to difficult at the time! "Who are you"? she asked. "I am the

Holy Spirit, that lives in your heart Ella" she was stunned "Why do you live there?" she asked "I come to council and comfort you and all people who will accept me and Jesus and those that know God is the mighty Creator of the Universe and all in it." "Shoo-oo I never knew that" said Ella. "Well now you do and so I am going to ask you a question—Do you accept us, known as the trinity . . . The Father, Son and Holy Spirit Ella. "Oh yes I do because my little Angel told me that God sent the storm to give me a way to escape. YES!! YES!! I DO . . . I know it is true. Will you always stay with me like my little Angel does . . . . PLEASE!!" "Yes Ella I will never leave you" then she fell asleep again for many hours.

Chapter 2

Ella stayed in that area for a long time as she had discovered a river close by her new home. There were also some fruit trees not far from the bush that she lived under. There were also some guinea fowl and Ella used to take their eggs and let the raw eggs slide down her throat. Between the eggs and the fruit and the water from the river she managed to survive all summer.

Ella used to dance and sing her praises in the sunlight, and give thanks to the great wonderful spirit God and also to her little Angel.

As time went by Ella realized that she would have to look for somewhere else to stay as the winter was on its way. There was a chill in the air in the day time but the nights were getting colder all the time. She was sad that she would have to leave this place, where she had been happy for the first time in her life.

At dawn the next morning she started to make plans to leave and go in the direction that all the birds were flying in. She knew that the birds went away from the cold winter and stayed in warm areas until the summer returned, then they came back to build their nests and Mate.

Ella decided that she was going to leave immediately, and set off singing her little Angel song as usual, but she felt bilious and had a headache so she rested at intervals. She realized that there was something else wrong now, as her clothes were getting so tight that she had to tear the one side of her dress all the way down in order to feel comfortable in it. She thought that she had out grown it and had got fat from all the eggs and fruit that she had so freely eaten. Only then did she realize for the first time that she did not have the usual flow of blood for quite a while now. Ella let out a heart rendering scream, as she realized just what that meant. She burst into tears, and sobs that shook her to the very core . . . . Ella was all alone and pregnant.

Ella started to pray and asked her little Angel to please ask God, once again, to help her out of this dreadful situation. She said "what did I do wrong that this should happen to me?" Suddenly the voice of the Holy Spirit came and said Ella sweet child of God, you have not done anything wrong. It was the others who wronged you" "God is your vindicator and they will all receive their punishment according to his judgment and his will be done in his divine order and time". She knew that she was a victim of abuse because of the drunken lust of men and she felt the anger and hate building up inside of her for all of them but mostly for her father, who was responsible for all the men who had raped her over the past two years. Ella cried herself to sleep wondering which of those dirty rapists is the father of the poor innocent little baby she that she was carrying.

Early the next morning Ella set out to find a new home. She did not know where she was, nor in which direction she was going, so she said this prayer. "Angel's please protect me and guide me to a safe haven for the winter. Please send someone to help me out of this predicament. Thank you in the name of the Father, the Son and the Holy Spirit—Amen" Feeling much comfort after her prayer she knew that God in his infinite mercy had a plan for her and she would be safe. Ella lay down to rest for awhile as she seemed to get tired very quickly now. After a short nap she woke up with the sound of the wind whistling around her. This made her get up and go on until she found a place to hide from the wind, and the sand blowing everywhere around her. "Help me Angels . . . please help me" was her constant plea.

After she had walked for a long while she saw a change in the landscape. On the horizon she could see a mountain with trees and she started to run as fast as her now heavily swollen body and bleeding feet would permit. However she had to slow down and rest ever so often and darkness was falling on the earth and the night was almost here, but she finally got to the foot of the mountain. She rested again and while she was lying down she saw another bush, not very unlike the one that she had found before. Ella shouted "Thank you God and my Angels and thank you my precious Holy Spirit", and got up and went to the bush that was not far away. This bush seemed to reach the ground on the one side but there was an opening that she could get through if she crawled, which she did with much difficulty and then she fell asleep for the night.

At the crack of dawn, Ella got up to view her surroundings and search for water and something to eat. She saw a stream that seemed to come from the top of the mountain ending up in the river not far off. Gratefully she went to the stream to drink the clear sparkling water and then to look for food. There seemed to be nothing anywhere. She was almost about to give up and take a rest when she rounded a bend and a sudden movement caught her eye and she saw some small bushes with berries that she had never seen in her life before. Well if the birds were eating them to give them strength for their very long flight, then surely she could also. They were sweet and had a lovely flavor so she ate until she was satisfied. Now she had a home again, water and some berries, this would do fine until she could look around again the next morning. Maybe she would find some more things to eat when she had rested and had more strength to search in the area of her new found home.

Chapter 3

In the morning Ella bathed in the river, and rinsed her dress, then put it on the grass in the sun to dry. She wondered just what she could do to cover herself now as the dress only covered her on the one side and the top was so tight that she struggled to get it on and off. She lay down and stared at the sky and counted the clouds as they passed overhead. She had an idea now, there was a cloud in the sky that parted and the two parts drifted away from each other. Yes! That is the solution to the problem. I will tear the top off she thought, and turn the dress around when it opens out into one piece, then I can tie it around my waist to keep my stomach covered, and that is what she did.

She then found some wild baby spinach, broke it up into small pieces and ate them raw. They were just what she needed. The following day when she went to gather some more spinach she saw two nanny goats with kids feeding from the spinach patch. At first she wanted to chase them, but then she got a wonderful idea. If she could get closer to them daily, they might accept her and slowly but surely she could get some milk from them. Yes! She would try—starting now. Ella walked slowly towards them and to her amazement they just went on grazing as if she was not even there. When she stroked them it seemed that they were used to the human touch. Slowly she lay next to one and got close enough to pull the teat and aim the milk directly into her mouth. This she did daily for a week and felt the strength coming back into her body.

On a very cold day while she was getting her milk, she heard someone shout "Hey you there by my goat!" Ella almost died of fright "Come here at once!!" then she saw a very old woman standing in front of her "What do you think you are doing with my goats, you have no right to steal!!" she broke off in mid sentence when Ella stood up. "Oh my you are going to give birth very soon by the look of you . . . where do you come from?" "Do you mind if I sit down and talk to you auntie" Ella asked politely. The old women agreed but told her to follow her. She led Ella around the side of a huge rock and into a small cave and there Ella told her life story to the old hermit woman. She just shook her head and made clicking noises with her tongue. The old woman told Ella that much the same thing had happened to her and that she had also run away from home. She had been living alone here ever since.

Her name was Ester and she asked Ella to stay as long as she wanted to and said she would help her when the time came to give birth. They got on well together and told each other stories and joked and laughed. The next few days passed in blissful contentment for the two of them and they happily went about their chores.

During the night of the full moon Ella's water broke, and the labor pains started. Somewhere in the distance they could hear a wolf howling, and then another one, and then more and more joined in the eerie sounds, but there was one howl that was not eerie but very soulful. This was the one that worried Ester. She knew that when it was full moon and the wolf pack's got together and howled as they did now, there was one human being about to be born that would be a Lycanthrope. This was why there was just one wolf that had a soulful howl. It was the Akela of the pack and it had also been born a Lycanthrope. Neither completely human nor wolf, and it would only be the Akela while the moon was full. During this time all the wolf packs would assemble and would cower in fear of the mighty powerful ferocious leader of all the packs. However the Akela had to turn and leave its kingdom and surrender its powerful position before the night that the moon was no longer completely full. This was because it would soon shape-shift from ware-wolf back into its human physicality. If that had to happen when it was with the pack they would immediately kill and eat it. So yes it had a soulful howl partly in empathy for the baby that was about to be born, and partly because it longed for the company of a soul Mate.

Ester felt sick at the thought that if Ella was the only one that was going to give birth in the vicinity to-night then according to legend her baby would be a Lycanthrope. Ester cried silent tears and silently asked "Why God? Why? Has this dear little girl not suffered enough in her young life?"

Chapter 4

Ester took some of the goat skins that she had piled up in the corner of the cave, for Ella to **give birth on. She had many dried skins from the goats that had died over the past 50 years.**

Yes, that is how long she had lived there, that is how long she had been alone and free to do as she pleased. The labor pains were not so severe and frequent yet, but Ester knew what the poor little girl had to go through, and just how much she would have to suffer She brought water with a herb in it, this she knew would help to calm her, and slightly ease the pains as they got stronger. She sat next to Ella and held her hand, all the time Ester sang songs that she could remember, just to try and help her to relax.

The contractions started to come more regularly now, and they got worse with each one. Ester was very concerned because Ella's water had broken quite a while ago, and she knew that this was going to be a very painful dry birth.

She stared out of the cave entrance, remembering her own confinement, and tears welled up in her eyes. Her baby was a boy and the joy of her life, he was a delightful child and played around in the area of this very cave. When he turned 8 years old he started to venture further away when looking for berries and shooting rabbits with his sling shot. On one of his excursions he was bitten by a snake and tried to get back to his mother, but died among the rocks and shrubs on the mountain from the potent and fast acting venom, still holding a grouse in his hand. It took Ester three days to find him, and then she knew why he never came home with something for the cooking pot, as he usually did. Her heart was broken and she held and hugged him for what seemed to be hours sobbing and shouting on the top of her voice at God for being so merciless and cruel to her and her son. After all they had never harmed anything and only killed birds, grouse, and rabbits for their own nutrition and survival. Ester carried his now ridged little body back to the cave and prepared it for interment, wrapping her darling child in the softest skins that she had. She then placed his body on his bed in the cave while she dug his grave and then buried him under his favorite tree near the cave entrance.

While deep in thought she felt Ella grip her hand very hard and scream as she felt the contraction that was the start of the very painful labor now. The contractions were closer together and the indescribable pain was just about all that the poor little girl could bear. Ester sang softly while dabbing her sweating forehead, all the while Ella clutched her hand moaning and pleading with her to take the pain away. The sun was starting to set and Ester had to use two stones and some dry grass with which she started a small fire to boil water in a type of calabash. She also lit a branch of a bush that had an oily consistency, it would burn slowly and give her the light she would need once darkness fell. Ella screamed again and Ester ran to her side and took her hand, she held on to Ester so tightly that her nails dug into her flesh. Ella's back arched and a crescendo of convulsing agony came from vocal cords she never knew she had. Ester told her to squat and push hard whenever the contraction came. She stood behind her and put both her arms around her chest bringing her backwards to lean on Ester's knees, for support. She started to pant to get breath and then the screaming started again. "Push hard now Ella" "I am, I can't do it any more I am sore and tired" "You must push again now . . . as hard as you can" Ella got a surge of strength and she knew that it was help from her Angel's as she was too exhausted to push anymore. "Push now Ella . . . as hard as you can" She bore down with a terrific effort and beads of sweat broke out all over her body. Ella was very dizzy and the pain was unbearable, but Ester kept urging her to push down hard.

There was a gush of thick red blood and she felt as though her bones were breaking and that she was pushing all her insides out. Ester told her to lie down and rest, so she did, but just then she got another pain and bore down with all her strength, and Ester saw the head was stuck in the narrow birth cannel. She got a knife and made a slit to stretch it a bit. Then Ester took the head in both her hands and pulled for all she was worth. It was over at last and with that last pull and push Ella lapsed into unconsciousness.

The baby never cried and Ester was almost sure that it was dead, so she quickly put another goat skin over Ella to keep her warm. Then she picked the baby up and went over to the light to get a good look at it. OH!!!!!ooooooo, NO!!!!!oooooo, she wept tears at the sight of the little thing that Ella had just given birth to. How could she tell her that it was born dead, never mind let her see it. This little thing was so deformed that it did not look human at all. There were no eyes, one ear, only two holes where the nose should have been and the rest was just a large lump of a liver like thing, covered in clumps of thick dark hair. Absolutely no sign of a gender at all . . . . it was just a thing, one could not say what it was except not human, just a large livery lump with a deformed head!!!!

Ester took it and put it at the back of the cave, while she decided just how to tell Ella when she woke up.

She sat and wept for the poor thing and it's mother, then she got up to make a herb tea to give Ella that would help calm her and lessen the pain she was sure to be in. Just as she started to get the herbs ready, Ella woke up with the most dreadful scream. Ester thought that she could not have seen the thing in the dark, so what had frightened her so much? In an instant she was at Ella's side.

"What is wrong?" she asked," ooooh Auntie that pain is here again ".

That is not possible the birth was all over she thought, but examined Ella, and felt her stomach contract." AYE!eeeee Ella there is another one coming, we will have to do as we did the first time" Ella squatted with Ester's help and the procedure was repeated, after which Ella passed out once again. Ester thanked God for the blessed oblivion that would keep her pain free until she woke up again. She picked the baby up to look at it in the light and almost passed out her-self, the little thing's twin had been born. No! It was not the same she felt it move and it was very hairy, she took it out into the moon light to have a good look at it. Then it wriggled and started snarling and Ester got the fright of her life and dropped it. Only just minutes old it had shape-shifted into what it was . . . . the soul Mate of the soulful howling ware wolf. Already ferocious it ran into the cave smelling the fresh blood of its deformed twin, and there before Ester's eyes it began to devour the piece of whatever it was, and biting and shaking it, it started to gulp down pieces of the flesh until it had eaten the whole thing.

Obviously full and satisfied it ran straight to its mother and curled up next to her, and went to sleep.

Ester went out of the cave and climbed a little way up the mountain, where she could just let vent to all her pent up feelings. Then she let out a howl that was almost wolf like, and shook her fist up in the air, as if to show God just how sad and angry she was. Not just at what had happened to Ella, but also what had happened to her all those years ago. Ester screamed and shouted and jumped up and down, weeping all the time, until she was so exhausted, that she almost collapsed. Suddenly it started to rain and she ran back to the cave. She saw that Ella was still asleep and dried herself, then lay down next to her and the little ball of fur, if Ella had to go through all this trauma she was not going to go through it alone then Ester quietly spoke to God.

"Dear Lord only you know why all these things happen! only you can, heal the body from pain and only you can give me the right words to say to Ella and only you can make her understand, I am tired Lord, now I want to sleep, I leave it in your hands, Good night . . . . Ahhhhh to-morrow is another day" she said yawning quite a few times. There was silence in the cave, except for the sound of two very tired people breathing. Then the storm broke and hail, thunder and lightning, were causing havoc outside. It was just as though God himself was angry, at all the injustice that had been the cause of so much grief and pain . . . . YES MAN'S INHUMANITY TO MAN!!! OR SHOULD I SAY TO WOMAN? WHAT ARE YOU GOD? SPIRIT MAN OR SPIRIT WOMAN? AND WHY? WHY? WHY?

Chapter 5

The worst night of Ella's life came to an end and the sun streamed into the cave entrance. morning had broken. To-day is another day and Ester wondered just how Ella was going to react when she saw what had been inside of her all those months and what had caused all that excruciating agony last night. Oh, well she had left it in God's hands last night and it is still there now, she would have to wait until Ella woke up, to see how each hour unfolded. Right now she needed to find something for them to eat and milk one of the Goats. This poor dear little girl was going to need good nutrition and a lot of nursing before she would heal and be whole again.

She killed a guinea fowl with a sling shot and gathered some spinach and a root that she knew was very filling, as she had always eaten them in the past. She peeled the root and broke the leaves into pieces, these they would eat raw. Then she plucked the guinea fowl and disemboweled it, chopped off the head and put a thin branch right through it. The small fire was burning just at the right temperature and Ester placed the bird over the small flames. Both ends of the branch were supported on two Y shaped branches on either side of the fire. She had to sit near to it because she had to keep rotating the bird so that it would cook evenly Ester started to think about how she was going to tell Ella when she woke up, because the first thing she would ask for were her babies. "Oh God, please help me find the words, because I can think of none that could console this poor little mother".

The time that Ester was dreading came just at that moment, and she heard Ella's weak voice calling her name. She took the bird off the flames and went into the cave. "Good morning my little one, how are you feeling?" asked Ester. "Auntie I am very sore and so thirsty, please can I have some water" "Yes I will bring you some herb water that will quench your thirst and also take away the pain, I won't be long sweetie Ester took the water to Ella and helped her to sit up and drink, but as she sat up she grunted and it was a guttural sound, that came from deep in her throat . . ." OH!! it is too sore to sit Auntie, it is so very sore something is wrong down there, AWWW "Ester knew why, so she explained just what happened, and how she had to cut her to get the babies out.

"Please do not worry Ella I will make a poultice from the omega herbs and put it on you, I will do this every few hours for the next few days and then three times a day. It will take a very long time to heal, but it will, I promise you. You will have to lie down until it is better"

Ester dropped the water into Ella's mouth a bit at a time until she had finished it all. Then she asked her if she was hungry. "I have prepared a special dinner for you to-day little one, and I hope you will enjoy it". "Thank you Auntie I know it will be very nice and yes please I am hungry"

"Auntie where are my babies?" asked Ella" Will you please bring them to me? ", the dreaded moment had arrived! Now the little ball of fur moved yawned and climbed up on to Ella's chest.

"Oh! Auntie look how sweet" she said stroking this cute little pup and then gave it a kiss on the nose and cuddled it in her arms. Ella smiled and laughed as the little thing responded by licking her on the nose and wagging its tail.

Ester sat down next to Ella and stroked her arm," Sweetie, there is something that I must tell you about those babies" "Oh! Auntie you look sad, are my babies dead?

I am sure that they are because I am big and I almost died, so how could those poor little ones go through so much trauma and live? I am right Auntie hey? They are dead!!"

With tears in her eyes Ester nodded, then softly whispered "This is very difficult to explain sweetie, I will do the very best that I can but I do not know if you will be able to accept the truth" The little pup began to wag its tail and started licking Ella all over her face, and Ella laughed and hugged the pup, saying "We will have to find a name for you dearest little one may be we must call you Fluffy" and Ester answered her by saying "I think that you must wait a while and give it more thought my sweetie as she won't always be fluffy you know."

Ester explained right from the beginning to the end in great detail all about the births, and how the cute little fluffy one had eaten the badly deformed hematoma twin. Then she told Ella all about the legend of the Lycanthrope, and that the fluff ball is actually her daughter who would shape-shift back into the human body once the moon started to wane, and then shape-shift back into a were-wolf every time there was a full moon.

Ella stared wide eyed and open mouthed at the dear fluffy pup that had now curled up into a ball on her lap and was fast asleep. "You see Auntie just how wise God is, he knew that they came from the seed of very bad men and they would grow to be bad like the drunken swine that made them. Auntie you know God also knew that it was not my fault and he knows that I cannot look after them. He knows that I have no home to give them, and he knows everything that we do not know. God has many secrets and we must pray and ask him to tell us how we must live now, "Don't you also think so Auntie? "Ester agreed with Ella and said a silent prayer to the Holy Spirit, thanking him that he had given Ella the intuition that she had." You know Auntie that is why my babies were born to be as they were because God knows that there are too many bad people here now and he does not want anymore, that is why, I know Auntie, I know".

Ester was stunned at Ella's reaction and her little prayer, this was no ordinary young girl, this was a girl born for a destiny that only God had planned. Yes God has a plan for her life, but these circumstances were certainly not part of it that's for sure. What had happened in her oh, so young life, was the influence that the devil had on the drunken lustful sod's that had taken advantage of her and abused her, with the encouragement of her unforgivable father. All the pain and suffering that his daughter had to endure and for what!!!! his convenience and his wanton life style. I hope they all burn in a hell so hot that it makes molten lava seem like ice, thought Ester. All the time that Ester was deep in thought, Ella had been staring at the sleeping ball of fluff that she had given birth to and was trying to find a word to describe it. Was it a wolf in sheep's clothing, or a sheep in wolf's clothing?

All she could come up with was "DEVIL THING". When Ester heard her utter those two words she stopped thinking about what was and focused on the here and now and what still had to be done. "Auntie do you think that this one ate the other one so that we would not have to put it in Gods good earth, and make it bad?" "Well that is the best that we could have done sweetie" "Auntie if we burnt it in a big fire so nobody would ever know about it, then it would have made all the fresh air bad, and that's even worse, ... Oh! Auntie it is better that this one ate the other devil thing. Oh! what are we going to do with this one now?

I want to forget all about them. I don't want to even remember that they were born, and I want to forget all about the life that I have lived so far . . . . do you think I can do that?" "Well Ella you can try to put it all out of your mind, by not thinking about it every day, but there will always be something at sometime that will remind you of what happened, and then there is this fluff ball that needs a name." Please take her away from me Auntie, I do not want to hold her anymore". Ester moved towards Ella with her hands held out to take the child-pup and it jumped in the air and savagely growling bit off Ester's right index finger and ate it, then it went and curled up on Ella's lap and promptly fell asleep again. Ella was hysterical and threw it off of her lap, but it came back and playfully started licking Ella's face again.

To this pup it was just having fun with its mother and the reaction was repeated a number of times, while Ella screamed until she fainted. Ester although in severe pain and bleeding profusely, tried in vain to get it away from Ella, but it kept snarling and snapping and showing its teeth until Ester backed away and went to attend to her wound.

In the distance but very much closer now there was a single soulful howl that continued until rosy streaks of light heralded the dawn of yet another troubled day.

After she had rested for a while, Ester gave Ella some food and more herb water and changed the poultice, while the pup slept at her feet.

Ella was in pain, physically, emotionally, and spiritually but she was very brave, and always had a smile for the dear old lady. Now the sun was high in the sky and from the foot of Ella's bed there was a pitiful cry . . . the cry of a human baby.

Ester and Ella both looked at the baby dreading what they were going to see. There at the foot of the bed was the most beautiful perfect little baby girl. They both gave a sigh of relief and Ester picked her up and put her in Ella's arms. With tears streaming down her face Ella looked at her daughter and said, "God forgive me but I cannot love you the way that I should.

It is not my fault nor is it your fault that you were born to be what you are. Baby girl all that I can promise is that I will do the very best that I can to be a good Mother to you" Ester spoke now also with tears streaming down her face, "God knows that my sweetie and your Angels will help you to learn to love her with both of her personalities and they will help me too. Now you must think of a name for her, and you must remember that there is a lot in a name so try to find a very nice one for her. I am sure that her name will influence her were-wolf animal instincts and they will not be so vicious and ferocious when she has to shape-shift each time." "I will do my best Auntie but will you please also think of a nice name as I do not know many names and their meanings?" "Yes Ella if you want me to, I will also do my best but as you know I have not heard any names since I came here over fifty years ago! There is no hurry as she is just new born but we must have one before the next full moon!"

Chapter 6

One day she asked Ester "Auntie you have been so good to me, just like a mother should be, but I cannot remember my mother because she was stabbed to death by my father when I was only three. One night when he came home drunk my mother shouted at him and he just picked up the bread knife and murdered her. My older brother told me about how she died and showed me where my father buried her. Auntie can I please call you mommy? Ella, you can if you want to, and you will be my daughter but I would like to call you sweetie, is that O.K." "That will be very nice, thank you, mommy" Ella had never kept time, days and weeks and months turned into years and she never knew when her birthday really was.

The family never celebrated birthdays and not one of them knew when it was. Unbeknown to Ella to-day was her birthday. Her 16th birthday!!, and this was the day that God choose to give her a new mother.

That night Ella said a prayer and thanked the Holy Spirit, and her Angels for giving her a mother that cared for her and loved her, and for the home she now had. Then she went to sleep, and she felt like a brand new person when she woke up. She felt so new that she said," Holy Spirit I feel like I have just been born again. Thank you and my dearest Angels, for guiding me and showing me the way to this wonderful, wonderful place".

Ester came in bringing Ella some herb tea and fruit that she had just picked from the cactus that Ester named prickly pears because they had thorny prickly spikes on them and were very difficult to peel." Good morning sweetie how are feeling now?" she asked. "I feel much better thank you mommy, and the baby girl is smiling and gurgling, just look how happy she is" "Yes I see, but have you thought of a name for her yet? As you know it will soon be full moon again my sweetie" "No mommy I cannot think of any that will suite her, but have you got any yet?" "Yes I have thought of just one that is appropriate but you will have to agree otherwise we will have to begin again! The name that I thought of is a Latin name, it is Nona and it means fate. Then if you reverse the letters it will be Anon and it means unknown. So I thought Nona would be perfect because it means "Fate Unknown" as we cannot determine her destiny, poor little thing" "Oh! Mommy that is perfect we will name her Nona and take her down to the river and baptize her right now, will you please honor her by doing that. If she is baptized maybe her destiny will change and not be so cruel when she has to shape-shift every time. Maybe then she will have someone to protect her just like our guardian Angels protect us." Then they went down and baptized her as "Nona".

Ester and Ella went about their chores, everyday they harvested what was available in the area and collected eggs from the fowl that nested not far from the cave. They milked the goats and drank as much milk as they wanted. Now Ester told Ella that it was time to learn how to make goat cheese with the preserving herbs that she had always used. All the things that Ester used in daily living she had got from trial and error over the years. Ester was a good teacher and Ella mastered all the tasks that she was given. The night of the full moon was fast approaching and Ester and Ella were expecting the dreaded event of the Lycanthrope, the time when an afflicted human shape-shifted into the werewolf. A vicious and ferocious creature that would stop at nothing until it had satisfied the cravings and yearnings of its intense and extremely wild nature. They both felt quite sick at the thought of this beautiful little girl turning into a wild creature, and just how big she would be. Would she turn on them and devour them as she had done to her deformed hematoma twin moments after she had been born, and also the way that she had bitten Ester's finger off and eaten it, neither of them could forget that. They began to be filled with fear as the time approached.

The days were very hot and staring into the far distance one could see a mirage forming that mirrored the thoughts in one's mind and the longings of one's heart in some instances. As they sat there eating berries and drinking the cool stream water Ella asked "Mommy do you see a mirage with two people in the distance or is it just my imagination, because no one ever comes here it is so far away from civilization and rural populated areas?" "Yes Ella I also see it and I doubt if this is a mirage my sweetie, I think that it is just what we are both seeing two people in the distance coming towards us!" "Mommy should we go into the cave so that they cannot see us?" "No sweetie we must sit here and see who they are and where they come from and what they want." Now they waited with bated breath as the two came ever closer to them. One was a grown woman and with her was a boy of about five years old, they could see that the woman was limping and also leaning on to the boy's shoulder for support. Ester said "stay here sweetie I must go forward to greet them and welcome them for a meal and some cool water as they have come from far and must be thirsty and hungry you know."

They stood still as Ester approached so she waved and shouted "Hello there you are welcome here come with me to my home and rest from your weary journey, and have something to eat and drink." The woman waved back and replied "Thank you that is very kind and we are very grateful." "I am Ester and I live here in a cave with my daughter Ella and grand-daughter Nona." then the woman introduced herself and the boy. "I am Prudence and this is my son Justice, we have come a very long way and cannot thank you enough for your kindness and hospitality dear Ester." The introductions having been done they proceeded on to the cave where Ella was waiting with Nona in her arms. Ester presented Ella and Nona with great pride and joy to the eager visitors and then they sat down to a meal of spit roasted grouse and sweet wild young spinach with goat cheese mixed berries and cold clear stream water. The hunger and thirst that had ravaged them for days that seemed like weeks had been sated and now they leaned against the cave wall with smiles on their faces and both said" We thank the great creator and also you the providers for the best meal that we have ever eaten."

"I think that it is time for me to explain why we are here and also the reason for my unfortunate deformed appearance," said Prudence. "I had the misfortune of being born under the influence of the full moon while a pack of wild wolves in the near vicinity were howling, and years later so was my son Justice, therefore we were both afflicted with the curse of the Lycanthrope that shape-shifts into a werewolf with every full moon. Living the life of an outcast neither human nor animal, not accepted by anyone and always nomads because we have no home. It is almost time for the full moon again and so we will have to take to the lonely wilderness and defend ourselves against all odds. Once when I was in the werewolf form I waited to long to back down to the pack Akela and at sunrise I turned human again, but it was to late to run and was savagely attacked by the wolf pack that I had dominated just hours before. As you can see I was badly wounded but not killed. Saved by the rifle shot of a deer hunter as it had scared the pack and they dispersed. I was left with half a foot many deep bites that had torn flesh from my body, and just one eye and a broken jaw. Luckily there was a river nearby and I just waded into it and swam across, so as to have a boundary of defense between them and me. Slowly and painfully I healed into what I have become and therefore would be even less accepted by humankind, not that I wanted to go near them because of my cursed destiny. Five years ago I came across an abandoned human baby and so I took care of him and named him Justice as that is just what I wanted for this dear little one and so he became my son. I knew that my human motherly instinct would stop me from harming him.

When the first full moon was high in the sky I felt myself starting to become a werewolf and was suddenly surprised by the yapping of a young werewolf running up to me. That is how I discovered the reason why his mother had abandoned him, and we have been together ever since with compassion and empathy for each other. The spirit of my human and animal higher self tells me that you have also given birth to one like us Ella, am I right or wrong dear sweet innocent young girl that you are?" Ester replied to her question confirming it to be true, as bitter sad tears ran down Ella's face and she sobbed uncontrollably. Prudence went over to Ella and hugged her and comforted her with words that only one who had experienced the same cruel fate could possibly do.

The next morning at breakfast Prudence looked up at the sky and said "We will have to leave now as to-night the full moon will spread its luster all over the earth and the wolf packs will gather from all directions and howl, some with aggression and some will have the soulful howl of the Lycanthrope. Will you entrust Nona to Justice and I and let her go with us during this time and we will bring her back when it has passed please Ella, for her sake and yours.?

Ester encouraged Ella to give Nona to Prudence and Justice and with a wave good-bye the three went off into the oncoming evening hours.

Ester and Ella did their chores as usual but in silence and then had something to eat and drink after which they went into the cave and huddled together saying prayers for the protection of the three who would have to face the consequence of their cruel fate that night and every night while the moon was full. They thanked God and the Angels that Nona was not alone and would always have a defender when necessary. Every day they sat at the cave entrance waiting for the three to return, and then unexpectedly one day they heard Prudence's familiar voice hailing them but it came from behind them, in the same direction that Ella herself had come. They jumped up and ran around to the other side of the cave and there were the three dear people that had left a short while ago. Much hugging and joyful laughing ensued and Prudence put Nona into Ella's eager arms. Then they all went back inside and had a meal and goats milk. That night their situation was discussed in depth and at length and it was unanimously decided that Prudence and Justice would live with them and that the three would come and go as the moon dictated.

They all lived happily and carefree together for the next ten years. They were very blessed to have this time together, and they enjoyed every moment of it.

Chapter 7

One day Ella noticed that Ester was not her usual self, and kept a watchful eye on her without her being aware that she was doing this. She saw Ester go up the mountain and followed her. Then she saw her lay down for quite a while in the shade of a large tree. Suddenly she got up and started vomiting, and then lay down again. This went on for a few days before Ella asked her what was wrong. "Mommy I think that goat milk is to rich for you now, because I have seen you throwing up, maybe you must not have so much anymore, what do you think? Eater looked into Ella's eyes, and then she said, "Because you have seen this I think that I must explain something about this vomiting my sweetie!" "Yes please mommy tell me what is wrong with you, and I will try to make you better." "Thank-you sweetie, but there is nothing that will make me better now, I am old and now I am dying, soon you will have to bury me" "NO! NO! NO! You can't die mommy, I need you so much, NO! NO! NO!"

"I know sweetie, and I am sorry to leave you, but the Great Spirit God, is calling me home!! It won't be very long now, but you are a grown woman and have learned very well how to live from the abundance of the good land here. The Holy Spirit and the Angels will look after you as they always have, and you are not alone as you have Nona, Prudence and Justice living with you, so I am sorry to leave you all but I am comforted by the knowledge that you have a family"

Ella was so distraught that she went outside and one could only use the words "BAYED TO THE MOON" in anguish, there are no other words to describe the cry that she let vent to. With tears streaming down her face she fell onto her knees, with arms pointed to the sky, and pleaded her question to the Great Spirit God, the creator of all that is "Oh! God why has this got to happen now? Why must the only mother that I have ever known be taken from me? Why God why? . . . Angels . . . Holy Spirit . . . please oh please answer me . . . why, why, why?" Ella cried and pleaded like this on and on for what seemed to be hours, deep into the very dark night. Eventually her pleading and sobbing subsided, and she lay down on the very dry sandy ground, and stared blankly into the darkness that seemed endless. It seemed to encapsulate the world, and Ella wondered if the entire universe and all that had been created, was dark and that no light would ever penetrate it again.

A gentle breeze wafted over her, as she contemplated what the future would be like without her mommy Ester.

Along with the breeze came the sound of the voice that she knew so well, "Ella you must be told this so that you will never question the workings of the almighty again, sweet child of God. You already know that the Great Spirit works in a divine order, and in this order is also divine time. It is written that there is a season for everything, this has been proven to you with, summer, autumn, winter and spring. There is also proof that you were aided by this divine order, so that you could flee from your persecution and your abusers. Well this includes a time for living and a time for dying. When we have completed the Great Spirit's plan for our lives, then they have to come to an end and our bodies have to die and be put in a grave. But our spirit that lives in us never dies, it goes back to the source from which it came, because it was the part that was given to us when we were born. It kept us alive until our season had come. Now your mommy Ester's season is about to end, her time will soon be over, and you must go on to new experiences and a new life." Ella knew that it was true, because she knew the voice of her Holy Spirit, so she thanked him for teaching her, and knew that she could rely on him to help her, and she knew that her Angels would too. Now she heard voices calling her name and saw three silhouettes against the rosy colour of the sky as the sun started making an appearance above the distant mountain range. Had she been away from the cave for most of the hours after midnight she questioned herself.

When Prudence, Justice and Nona reached her half way to the cave she just ran into Prudence's open welcoming and comforting arms and burst into tears again. "Where have you been and what has upset you so much they all enquired?" "Let us sit down here and I will tell you all what it is." Ella proceeded to tell them all about Ester's terminal illness and that she would not be with them for very much longer. The news was devastating and saddened them all. Shocked into silence and with tears streaming down their faces they all got up and returned to the cave, fearing what each day would bring.

Ester was on her back and it seemed that she was finding it very hard to breathe, and when she coughed, blood came out of her mouth. This went on for days and days, and Ella and the family did the very best that they could to keep mommy Ester clean and comfortable. They also tried to make the food soft and cut up very fine, so that Ester could chew and swallow it, without much effort. Ella made the herb water to ease the pain that her mommy was in, and she added another goat skin on top of her, when she got cold. Ella also kept a vigil at her side all the time, but when she got too tired she laid down next to Ester, and put her arm around her to give her some comfort, and at the same time hold on to her as long as she could. Tonight they would cuddle up as always. Tomorrow was another day, and she wondered what the situation would be at sunrise.

Ella woke up at dawn and whispered to her Angel "Well to-day is the to-morrow that I worried about yesterday, what will this day bring?" She bent over to kiss Ester good morning, and felt that she was ice cold and rigid, her eyes were open but the life had drained from her.

Tears flowed from Ella's eyes, and she gently closed her mommy's dear kind loving old eyes having looked into them for the last time. She lay down next to her, and just sobbed and held her tightly in her arms. The loud sobbing woke the family and they went over to Ester and Ella only to realize that Ester's precious spirit had returned to the source of its genesis and now what remained was the dead body of their mommy Ester that they had all loved so very much.

They all prepared her body for burial enveloping it in the goat skins from the storage at the back of the cave.

The time had come to dig a grave for her and they chose a place right next to where Ester had laid her own son to rest, all those years ago. It was under the huge tree near the cave entrance, and there was always shade because of the angle that the branches grew at. It was a lovely peaceful spot and they knew that it was the best one that they could ever choose. Then Ella picked up egg sized stones until she had enough, and lovingly placed them on Esters grave. It simply spelled out two words "OUR MOMMY ".

Now they had to live a life without Ester and be content with doing little things that were just routine, day after day. However they were grateful for this home that their dear mommy had left them with, and all the food in the area, and also the goats, their milk and the cheese they had made. They planned to live there for the rest of their lives, free, happy, healthy and content just as their beloved mommy had, until their season came too. The months turned into years, and the years into decades. Then something happened that had never happened before and Ella was worried. There was no rain for months on end, and slowly but surely all the trees and bushes started to wilt and die, even the stream and the river dried up . . . there was nothing left to gather, and today when she went to milk the goats, she discovered that the goats had left to look for green pastures and a water supply. Just what were they to do they knew that they would have to leave as there was nothing left. Ella went and sat by Ester's grave and spoke to her for hours, all about the past, present and future. She unburdened every problem to her very, very, dear mommy, and then she went to sleep in the cave.

That night they could hear the wind howling around the cave, and knew that the swirling sand was cutting patterns into everything that was in its way. The wolves were also howling and together they made an eerie sound. Why were the wolves howling, there was no full moon, Ella decided that they must go the next day, and started to plan what was to be done in the morning. They collected some broken branches, and tied them together with strands cut from a goat skin. The structure she made was as long as she was tall, and very strong. On this she loaded all the goat skins and rabbit skins, the spade, calabash and knife some stones, and the four blocks of cheese that she had made from the goat milk. She made a handle out of a long strand that she attached to the structure, this Justice put around his neck and dragging it behind him they went to say a last good-bye to their "MOMMY" then once again set off into the vast unknown.

Chapter 8

They went along at a steady pace, all the time singing the "LITTLE ANGEL SONG" and then singing "PRAISE TO THE GREAT SPIRIT GOD FOR HE IS GOOD TO US, HE GAVE US A HOME AND HE SET US FREE" Now the sun was declining behind the mountain, and the moon's luminous light would be their solace, in a dark and lonely world.

When the moon was high in the sky they heard the creepy sound of the wolves howling far in the distance from which they had just come. It was an eerie ghostly feeling and Ella felt goose bumps all over her body. She wondered why because it had never affected her before. Little did she know that it was the wolves' intent that made her flesh crawl. There were four of them and they were thinking, "DRY OLD BONES WERE BETTER THAN NO BONES! As they were digging up the grave of the family's beloved mommy. They off loaded all the things and lined the branches with some goat skins they also covered themselves with some of them and used a few rabbit skins for pillows. Ella asked her little Angel to watch over the family and keep them safe while they slept. Then she said "Goodnight moon keep on shining" there were no stars out that night!.

In the morning they loaded their belongings, had some cheese, and started on the journey once again, to which end she never knew. She found out that the days were to hot so she decided to move only at night from then on and the family all agreed. They protected themselves from the sun with goat skins, and in the rain, and from the wind and the cold. Were goats not just the most marvelous creatures in creation? Ella asked herself. This was their way of life now but they had to find water soon as the moisture in the cheese was not enough to keep them hydrated. Maybe they would survive for a few more days. The sand was lighter now and more like small grains that filtered through her fingers. Also she could smell a salty type of scent, but she never knew what it was. They tried to keep an even speed, and they noticed that there were more up hills and down hills than ever before. Justice had to pull hard to go up and then had to run down the other side. So when on the down hills he turned the structure and let it go first then he ran behind it, laughing at the fun of it. Prudence looked up at the sky and said "Ella! Justice, Nona and I will have to leave for a while as there is a full moon on the way, but you must not worry because we will not go far just wait here for us and we will return as soon as possible." "I will do as you say Prudence and I hope that the moon will not be full for to long as it is lonely without you all."

That night the full moon was high in the sky and as usual was the luminary that gave light to the earth during the night hours. Then Ella heard the howling of the wolf packs as they assembled for the Akela of each pack to compete with the others not only to be the leader of the pack but also to increase his pack in numbers by defeating the Akela of another pack.

Not far from where she had taken refuge for the night she heard the terrible howling, snapping and snarling that ensued and she knew instantly that the fight for their lives had begun among all the pack wolves. Ella curled up into a ball and covered herself with some goat skins and was prepared to stay hidden in this way until her family returned. As the night hours went by one by one Ella listened to the howling and pitiful whimpering of those that had been badly wounded and she shed tears for them in their plight. Suddenly she was aware of warning snarls very near to her and peeped out between the goat skin coverings. What she saw made her blood freeze, their looking at her were two werewolves that were obviously on their way to the howling wolf packs in the vicinity. Ella held her breath and waited for them to lunge forward and devour her, and she was sure that her time had come, but did it have to end like this. In the awareness of her higher spirit self she could hear a celestial choir singing the words to a song that her mommy Ester sang to her while she was going to sleep every night. "I'll be loving you always, when the things you've planed need a helping hand I will understand always" the tears were welling up in Ella's eyes "Oh how I long for you mommy especially now as it seems that my time has come and I am all alone" her thoughts were broken off by the dreadful indescribable sounds of a fight right in front of her. Ella peeped out again and was witness to three werewolves fighting ferociously, and she knew that the lone werewolf would have to fight the other two and also that it would be a fight to the death. This battle went on for hours it was vicious and cruel, eventually one werewolf fell to the ground and was writhing in the agony of its death pangs, whimpering softly until death mercifully came. The other two carried on fighting briefly and then realizing that they were the victors ran off in the direction of the contesting wolf packs. When all was still around her hiding place Ella slowly crept out and crawled over to the dead werewolf. She looked at the terrible wounds that had been inflicted and at the pools of blood around it and then went closer and closer very slowly and carefully. When she got near to the head she almost fainted this was the one eyed wolf Prudence who had rushed in to save her and in so doing gave her own life to defend Ella from certain death.

Ella fell to her knees in the soft loose sand and took the torn broken and now lifeless body in her arms and hugged it mournfully sobbing and thanking Prudence from the depths of her very soul. She sat like that until the dawn broke the darkness of what had seemed to be a never ending night. Just then she heard two voices hailing her and waving, but she never waved back and instinctively they knew that something was wrong and they began to run towards Ella who was holding a werewolf in her arms. On their arrival they saw just one eye in the wolf's head and it was half closed. When the sun was high in the sky the dead werewolf body became a dead human body for the very last time. Three very brokenhearted people sat around their beloved Prudence in silence each with their own memories of the life that they had shared with her for so long.

Justice was the first to end the silence and said "We will have to bury her somewhere, but where? This sand is too soft and loose here and her body will become an easy target and meal for some marauding animal. No we will just have to look further ahead and see if there is a more suitable place." Over the sand dunes and just a short distance from where they were they saw the sea. Ella had a brilliant idea and told the others who immediately agreed. They used goat skins in which to enshroud her and put her on to the wooden sleigh that they had used to load and drag their belongings on from the cave. Justice put the goatskin handle around his neck and dragged it into the sea, swimming out with it beyond the breakers. Once he got to calmer waters he let it go and swam back to the beach, joining Ella and Nona.

They all said a prayer and sang hymns watching the makeshift raft until it was out of sight. Thunder clouds threatened to bring a storm and then bright blue and white lightning snaked along in the sky and it opened up and let the long awaited rain fall upon the parched earth, soaking it up like a sponge until it was saturated. Slowly rivulets began to form on the dunes and they ran into the sea, as did all those inland ones that came from the mountain ranges.

Ella, Nona and Justice danced in the rain thanking the Great Spirit for mercifully giving them rain and therefore hope to go on living with abundant food and cool clear water again.

In the morning it was still raining but very softly now and Ella knew that rain like this would last all through the spring and the summer and she felt very good. "I have no idea where we are but we are so far from the cave now that I suggest that we carry on and see where the spirit leads us." "No Ella I think that you should go on and see where the spirit leads you, but I think that Nona and I should return to the cave where we will have shelter and an abundance of food. It is not wise for us to go on and reach populated areas because of the curse that we are the victims of. It is a lifelong thing that we have to bear and thankfully together." With a broken heart but also agreeing with the wisdom that Justice had made his decision on, Ella gave them her blessing, telling a sobbing Nona that it was the right thing to do, and sadly waved to them until they were out of sight.

Chapter 9

Once again Ella was all alone, yes alone and with all her memories still a fugitive from her past. She walked for miles and miles and developed a thirst that needed quenching very soon.

As she walked she looked around and said "Water, water everywhere but not a drop to drink!"

Then as she rounded a bend she saw a river that went into the sea, and she went into it bodily and drank, and drank, and drank. She drank so much that she was sure to put any camel to shame.

When she was full she burped and thanked the Great Spirit God for his provision, and also for his mercy. That is when she heard the deep loud sound that rent through the air, and she jumped out of the river, and ran to see what it was that disturbed the silence, "What is that Ella shouted in absolute fear?"

Then she saw it . . . a huge ship that kept making that loud noise. Also there was the voice of her little Angel encouraging her as she did before. "GO! ELLA, GO NOW, THIS IS YOUR CHANCE TO LEAVE, GET ON THAT SHIP, GO NOW BEFORE YOU ARE LEFT BEHIND!!!" Her mind was made up in an instant, and she went silently and waited until there was no one near it, then she made a dash for the gangplank, and stowed away under the life boats, in the shadows where no one would see her. After a while some "SWINE MEN" pulled the gangplank up on to the ship, and it started to move. Slowly but surely it sailed away, and it was not long before the shore line was a mere spot, that faded into nothing. All Ella could see now was water, and as the sun came up with a beautiful rosy glow, she said a silent last goodbye to her mommy Ester, Prudence, Nona and Justice and fell asleep.

Ella slept all day and was a little surprised by her surroundings, when she remembered that she had got on this boat and now she was very hungry. She knew that she dare not try to leave her hiding place or those "SWINE MEN" would find her. There were so many of them and she tried not to think what would happen to her if she got caught. Those despicable years of childhood abuse and the pain inflicted on her by all those drunken devils, because of their lust, and her father's greed came flooding back and she almost drowned in the memories. All of a sudden one of the swine men walked away from the others, and headed in her direction. Ella crouched and cringed as he got nearer to where she was hiding. To her amazement he was dropping bits of bread while he was staggering around. She waited until no one was in sight and slid along on her tummy to pick some up. Sh'o! She was so very hungry. She stuffed this food into her mouth and swallowed with very little chewing. It tasted vile but whatever it was would relieve the hunger pangs. She went back into her hiding place and tried not to think of anything. Suddenly she felt dreadful pains in her stomach, then she vomited and passed out . . . . Ella had ingested rat poison

Once again her little Angel had protected her from the evil in the world that she lived in, by the constant abetting to flee. The hunger, thirst and fear together with the muscular tension that had built up in her urgency to escape from the things that were tormenting her, only to find that this ship was infested with "SWINE MEN" caused her solar plexus, to convulse and also her stomach. This was what caused her to vomit and in so doing she expelled what she had just eaten. This was in fact an act of mercy and it saved her life. She had been found while she was unconscious. The deck hand needed to clean under the lifeboats to see if the poisoned rats had died there, and he found Ella. He alerted the captain that there was a woman stowaway on his ship. On investigating this report the captain realized that she had eaten the bread. This fact was obvious from the contents of the vomit next to her.

He ordered some sailors to take this beautiful woman that was clad only in a goat skin tunic to the sick room and tell the ship's doctor to help her.

Ella woke up in a bed that had nice clean sheets on and knew that she had been discovered, she started to shiver in fear like she did as a child when she never knew what to expect. She saw that she had something in her arm and it was hurting. The doctor had inserted a drip in her right arm and it came from a little bag that was hanging above her, the liquid was clear, just like the sparkling water from mommy's stream she thought. Her left arm was also sore and she realized that there was another drip going into her arm, but this one had stuff like blood in it, and in her state of mind she thought that they were putting the swine blood back into her again.

Ella wanted to pull it out of her arm but they had tied her to the bed, and she could not move. She started to shout "Hey! Someone help me please?" Then she observed a man dressed in white sitting in the room, he came over to her. "Good morning ma'am, I am so pleased that you have woken up, I have been praying for you to recover with the help of this treatment" Ella looked at him with a frown, she thought, what! A swine man that said prayers, surely she had died and gone to heaven, because on earth they only drink and hurt woman.

She managed to stammer "Good morning, are you the doctor sir?" "Yes I am and now that you are awake I will untie your hand and leg restraints so that you can move a little" "I am so very sorry that I had to tie you down but you were fighting all the time and I had to keep you still for the drips you see, otherwise they would have come out and we could not help you without this treatment." Ella could not believe her eyes and ears, she must be dreaming, men were not like this on earth. This man was not from the same type that she was used to, she thought that all men were the same everywhere. "OH! Great Spirit please forgive me for judging your creation but you know I did it because the only men I knew were dirty and drunk and they abused me that was all I knew". Then her vision cleared and she could see the doctor. He was clean and had no hair on his face, and he spoke so kindly to her. Then she saw that his skin was like hers, light brown and he had the same blue eyes as she had. This was a godlike man yes indeed very special. Ella felt all the fear leave her . . . . she instinctively knew that she could trust him. This was confirmed when she heard the celestial singing and felt the comfort of the Holy Spirit with her"

Ella noticed that this handsome doctor looked at her in a very special way, it was so lovingly and he often smiled at her, when he was sitting behind his desk. Somehow she was aware of feelings that stirred her heart, in a kind of loving way when he smiled at her. The ship's captain asked the doctor how she was doing, and he just said I think I have a small chance of saving her." I hope so, she is a rare find, and a very beautiful one" and there was a hint of tenderness in his voice. This made the doctor worry that the Captain might have other ideas for this woman, but then so did he, so he derived a plan not to tell him that she was awake and that she had said a few words. When he went back to check on her, she was wide awake but kept her eyes closed until she was sure that it was only him in the room. Then she looked at him and he said "Hello there, are you feeling better?" she nodded and he took her hand to check her pulse. When he touched her she got strange feelings that she never had in her life before, it felt as though her whole body was set on fire, but such a nice fire, and she made a sudden unplanned exclamation, and started to tremble. The doctor smiled at her and asked" What is your name dear lady?" "My name is Ella, what is your name?" "I am Tom" he replied.

"Where do you live Ella, and why were you wearing a goat skin, and why are you running away? What are you so afraid of?" then he smiled that smile that she could not understand, and she started to tremble all over again." Tom I am going to tell you my life story, because I owe you my life, but you must promise never to repeat it to anyone please, do you promise?"

"Yes I do Ella, just tell me all of it, from the very start up to this very moment, I promise you it will remain, my secret, said Tom." That is when Ella told Tom everything that she had experienced. Her entire life history, came tumbling out, and all the time she was talking to him he listened intently, and with a look of such empathy, that Ella knew that she felt something very moving about him from deep inside her very soul. She was sure that it was love, but it was another kind of love, not the same as she had for her mommy Ester and the family.

While they were talking, Tom stretched with his arms up in the air, and Ella noticed that he had a plaster on his arm, where the bend was. "Did you hurt yourself there Tom?" she asked

"No I did not hurt myself Ella, it is where I took blood out of myself to put in that bag, so I could give it to you . . . we have the same blood group, you and I, so that is why I was able to give it to you."

Ella thanked him for all he had done to help her, and she blushed at the thought of this man's blood going into her, and going all over in every cell of her body. She decided right there and then, that this strange new feeling was love. OH! yes Ella knew that she loved him. He was now her Tom and she also knew that she never wanted to leave him. She just hoped that he would not send her off the ship, she would do anything just to be near him. "Ella you must be very careful now because if the Captain knows that you are awake then he will put you off at the next port, that is what happens to stowaways and the police will send you back home again. Keep your eyes closed when I am not here." "I will do that because the other men are not like you and I have been afraid of men all my life."

Chapter 10

The Ship went on sailing for days and days and Ella thought that this journey would never end. In one way she was pleased because she was with her beloved Tom, but then she was also worried that someone would find out that she was awake. The Captain had been in and out a few times to see how she was doing and then there was always the man that had found her in her hiding place. He came to clean the sick room and always stood and looked at her, and sometimes he said "Lady you must get better now see" she dreaded it when other members of the crew came in to check on how she was doing. Just by their voices and the things that they said, she could hear some "SWINE MEN" were among them. Ella got the creeps every time, but was thankful that Tom never left the room at visiting time. Tom had left the drip in her arm that had medicine in and also water, that is what it looked like to her. He shared his food with her so that the ships cook would count out the same amount of servings every day, making him a witness that she was not eating yet, just by the amount of meals served.

This routine went on for about another 10 days and then Tom told her that they were approaching the next port and that is when he intended to take her off the ship. He knew that the ship would be in the dock for a day and a night while the crew off loaded the cargo. It was also the port that he would get off to go on leave. Another Doctor would take over from him, and he would tell him that the woman must have escaped while he went to check on an injured crew member.

Just before it was time for the ship to dock there was a shuffling sound and Ella knew that it was a man entering her room by the sound of a cough that he made and then cursed at himself for coughing at the wrong time. This was the man that had found her and brought her to the hospital room. Very softly he said "Ah yes my little beauty, it was me that found you and so you are mine, I am going to take you and hide you and the Dr and the Captain will think that you have regained your consciousness and escaped" Ella started to get the shivers and found it difficult to hold back the tears that were welling up behind her eye lids. Suddenly the swine man let out a scream that brought others running to see what he was screaming about. While they were distracted Ella tried to peep so that she could also see what had frightened him so much. Then the others also started screaming and suddenly Ella knew why. There was a snarling sound coming from under her bed, and it got louder and sounded more ferocious when more sailors came to see what was going on, then suddenly and very unexpectedly this large wolf like animal lunged its self forward and they all turned and ran for dear life. Briefly it turned and looked at Ella and she saw that it had only one eye ! . . Prudence's werewolf spirit had materialized and had saved her from dangerous abduction. This was the second time that the one eyed werewolf had come to her rescue. The first time it had given its own life to save her now the werewolf spirit had materialized from the spirit world and saved her again. Softly she whispered "thank you my dear loving Prudence for what you have done for me ever since the day I met you, thank you Holy Spirit for bringing Prudence into my life" then she heard a noise and was aware of a presence next to her bed. Slowly she opened her eyes expecting to see Tom there, but it was not him it was Prudence in the spirit form of a human. "Ella dear child of God you and Ester gave us a home for many years and the Great Spirit God that created all things is going to reward you many times in the future. He has commanded me to be one of your protectors and I promise that I will always be watching over you, whenever you need me I will come it will not be necessary to call me.

I love you and I always will." Then she blew a kiss and went back to her spirit world. That night Tom took Ella off the ship while all were asleep and put her in a hiding place that he knew of, it was very safe and he would be back for her after he had handed over to the next doctor. Tom returned to the ship, and in the morning he told the story that he had made up.

All was agog now and every crew member and the police were looking for Ella but Tom knew that they would never find her. That evening the ship sailed and the captain left the stowaway's fate in the capable hands of the police, he was sure that they would find the woman, as she must be very weak and also she never knew this place at all and was not likely to go anywhere far from the harbor and the few small shops that constituted the whole town.

There was very little fertile ground in that vicinity, and then beyond in every direction other than the sea was desert as far as one could see and for many miles after that.

Tom said good bye to the police and the people that he had known for many years, and went in the usual direction that he took to go home, he went alone and they all waved good bye to him. When all was dark and quiet Tom went back to where he had hidden Ella and then they both left the town behind, and walked to Tom's home. Ella was so happy that all men were not "SWINE MEN" and also that she had found this wonderful handsome man, and that he had helped her to heal and escape. The two walked for hours and then Tom told Ella all about his life and how he and his brother had also ran away from a life of abuse. Their father had sodomized them and their older brother. When they ran away their brother was not at home and their mother was pregnant. Tom said that he supposed that they looked for them and then gave up. He told Ella that they were twins and were 5 years old when they made a run for it. These kind people found them wandering around and took them in. They also left on a ship with the family, to come to this place and it was here where their new father got a job, and they settled on a small plot of ground where they still lived.

Chapter 11

I t took two nights and a day to get to Tom's home. He called to his parents as they got near to the house, and his mother and father came running out to meet him. They threw their arms around his neck and kissed and hugged him. "Welcome home son, and who is this lovely lady that you have brought with you?" asked his mother." Mother this is Ella she stowed away on our ship. She was very sick and was trying to escape from the drought that had killed everything that there was to eat, and there was no water anymore. So they had to leave and look for somewhere to live". "Hello Ella, you are very welcome to stay here with us we have lots to eat and drink, come you two let us go inside". My name is Menlo and my husband is Jared, please sit and have some nice cold water, I am sure that you are very thirsty now".

The water was so very nice and cold Ella wondered how she kept it like that, and then she brought them some chicken pies that she had made and also homemade bread and delicious sweet jam, that she had made from the prickly fruit on the cactus that grew around their plot." Oh! thank you very much, I have not eaten so well in many years, I had forgotten all about pies, and bread and jam, thank you, thank you so much Auntie Menlo"

Another man stretched and yawned as he came into the eating and cooking room, and when Ella saw him she knew that this was Tom's twin, they were identical, no one could tell them apart. "This is Matt my twin brother, said Tom, and this is Ella" "Hello Ella where do you come from?" Tom interrupted and said "I think we must all sit down and let Ella tell you her life story, that will be O.K. hey Ella, will you do that?, tell them everything as you told me" "Yes I will, you are all so kind, and I am very grateful, thank you for taking me in, it is only right that you must know all about me." Ella told them her story, every little bit of it, everything right from her earliest memories. Menlo and Jared and also Tom and Matt had tears in their eyes, and at times Menlo sobbed. Tom wished that he was there to help her with the birth of what Ella called "DEVIL THINGS" and also to help Ester when she was so very ill, and when she crossed over to return to the Great Spirit. After she had told them everything, Menlo asked "What is your surname Ella do you remember it?" "Yes Auntie Menlo my surname is January" Hardly had she uttered the word when all the men stood up with a question "What did you say Ella?" Instantly there was a thump and when they looked Menlo had fainted. "This must be the baby Ma was going to have when we ran away Tom said to Matt!!"

Tom was attending to his mother, and dabbing her face with a cold cloth to bring her around, but felt like fainting himself. "Ella, Tom and I also have that surname, you must be our sister," explained Matt." Ella was dumbfounded, she was reunited with her twin brothers "How did this happen they all said together?" "It is the Holy Spirit, and the Angels that we must thank our reunion would never have happened if they never made it happen" "That is right Ella" said Menlo and we must all give thanks and praise to the Great Creator Spirit, and thank the Angels too. They all went on their knees and praised and thanked God and the Angels. Then they sang hymns that Ella never knew but she just kept saying "Thank you, Thank you, Thank you. Then it struck Ella that if Tom was her brother, then he would just have to stay her brother and so would Matt. Menlo gave Ella a bed to sleep on near the cooking room, and said "Ella you can also call me Mom and Jared Dad if you want to" "Yes I will be very happy to do so thank you for everything Mom". After saying goodnight to everyone she fell into a very deep sleep.

Early the next morning Ella woke up, and there was the most delicious smell of homemade bread, wafting in the air from the cooking room, and what she remembered as a brew called coffee. "WOW! I must get up and follow this 'HUNGRY SMELL'" said Ella. She went into the cooking room and found her new 'MOM' busy at the fire thing that she cooked on. "Good morning mom, something smells good enough to eat" "Good morning my darling, did you sleep well?" "OH . . . YES!!! It was the very best sleep that I have ever had thank you mom". "The family will be in here to eat shortly, sit down my child and have a nice cup of coffee and a rusk" When Ella saw the rusk, she vaguely remembered having put the end of one in the coffee and then eating it,' so many years ago. Everyone came into the cooking room, and sat down at the table, but not before they each gave her a kiss on the forehead. Dad started to delegate chores to the men, and asked Ella if she thought she could milk the cow. "I am sure that I can, I used to milk mommy Ester's goats, and also make cheese with the left over milk, I will do my best Dad". Then Menlo served her family a tasty breakfast of hot bread, jam, boiled eggs and coffee, after which they all went their separate ways to do the day's work on the plot.

Tears streamed down Ella's face as she started to milk the cow, it reminded her of the first time that she squirted the goat milk into her mouth, and also when she first met mommy Ester. Those bitter sweet memories of her mommy and all that she had taught her, in the cave days. There were also the ones that she had shut out of her mind, that wanted to surface again, but she just asked her little Angel to help her forget. Then she thought about Tom and how happy she was that he saved her life, and gave her this wonderful family and a safe comfortable home.

By now Ella was middle aged but looked twenty years younger, she was also beautiful and very strong, because of the fresh air and natural foods, and the fresh water that she had while she lived in the cave and the mountains. One day Matt looked at her as she scrubbed the floor and thought,' my poor little sister has never had the love of a good man, she has only known the hateful ones, I must do something about that'

"Tom we must find a good husband for Ella she is getting on in years, and I do not want her to have a lonely old age, she has had enough loneliness in her life, don't you think so too?" Tom agreed and a mutual decision was made.

Tom and Matt were both ships doctors and left after their time off, to return to duty, it would be another year before they where home again. Menlo, Jared, and Ella waved goodbye to them until both figures faded out of sight. Menlo and Ella wept silent tears, and Jared gave them both a comforting hug, then they went inside, for another cup of coffee and a chat about how the twins would be missed. Jared was old now and he found it very difficult to do all the heavy work that is necessary on a plot. Ella offered to keep the vegetable patch watered and weeded, and said that she would do the planting when the time came. She was taught all the ins and outs of gardening by mommy Ester, and had kept it up until the drought came, and she had to leave.

Menlo had pain in her hands and her fingers were twisted and remained in a downward position so that she could hardly lift a cup. Ella took over all the duties that her mom used to do. However she remained in pain, and Ella wished that she could find the plant that her mommy Ester had used to ease pain as it worked very well. All the time while weeding the vegetable garden, she was wondering why she never saw that plant growing here. It grew all year round at the cave and on the mountain. Jared told her that he was going into town to get a few things, and that it would take him about three days there and back. Ella packed a food parcel for him and also a bottle of water, that he could sip when he was thirsty.

He set off on his long walk to town in the early evening as it was cooler and he would get quite a distance before the sun's rosy glow appeared on the horizon. He intended to walk until midday then have a rest in the shade of that big rock that was in the middle of nowhere, as it was the only one and the only place that there would be some shade. He had rested there many times over the years that he did this trip to town.

Ella's mom was in more pain than usual that day and also complained that her knees were sore and swollen. This she had never mentioned before, she never complained, and if it was not for her twisted fingers she would not have said that they were sore. This was a fact that she could not hide from anyone. Ella decided that as soon as her dad was back home, she would go in search of mommy Ester's healing plant. The three days seemed to take a week in Ella's mind, and she was on a constant look out for her dad. "Great Spirit, and Angels please bring dad home safely and soon, we are missing him very much, and I have to go and look for that plant to help mom. That night while they were eating the door suddenly opened and there stood dad. He said that he had to rest for longer than usual, but he had brought something wonderful home for Menlo and Ella. He held his hand up in the air, clutching two paper things. Menlo started to cry, she knew that they were letters from her darling sons Ella could not read so Menlo read all the news to her from her brothers. Matt would be home in four months, but Tom's ship would be late as it had further to go, and it would only dock in another six months. They all thanked the Great Spirit that both the men were healthy and also for Dad's safe return.

The next day Ella set off to look for the healing plant. Somewhere she had to find a mountain and was sure there would be some plants growing there. She took food and water with her that would last for about a week, then she would have to return, with or without the precious healing plant.

Three days into her search, she realized that the sand was getting deeper and in some places she went knee deep into it, and it was very difficult to get far as she had to pull one leg out at a time and then the other one would sink in. This was getting very frustrating because she wanted to go as quickly as she could because she was on a mission to find the plant that would help her dear mom.

Ella decided to rest for a while and curled up in the fetal position as the wind started to blow and there was a very bad sand storm coming. It blew for ages and then stopped as suddenly as it had started. Ella went on walking and then realized that the sand was not so deep anymore, only up to her ankles so she hurried along to make up time. Her Angels had helped her without her asking this time. She thanked them, and sang a hymn that her mom had taught her.

Chapter 12

The days were so hot, Ella had gone through hot days before but never like this. When she looked into the far horizon, all she could see was a blinding haze, it looked like the air was on fire, and it felt like it too. This was a heat unknown to her, and it felt like her brain was roasting, and the little bit of fat on her body was melting off with the sweat as it just poured out of her. She went on and on and started to imagine that she saw a mountain and trees, and Oh! Yes there was water too. Ella staggered on towards this place but when she got there, there was only the endless sand. Was she going mad she wondered, and then she felt dizzy and fainted. After a while she woke up again and looked into the distance ahead, just the unbearable heat and the endless sand wherever she looked. Then all of a sudden she thought that her mind was playing tricks on her again. She was sure that she saw many camels, what did mom call them again. Oh! Yes mom had told her all about the camels that were called the ships of the desert. They went to a place to get salt for the nomad people of the desert. Mom said that some of them took months to get back to their tents where they had left their families. Oh! well she thought that this was just another one of those hazy things that she had seen earlier and then she passed out once again from the heat and utter exhaustion.

The ships of the desert that Ella had seen was a real caravan, of nomads on their return home, loaded with packs of salt. They found this woman just spread out on the sand far from any civilization. The man in charge told them to put her on his camel after he had made sure that she was still alive. That night Ella woke up to see a very starry sky and a full moon high above her. Somewhere in the distance she could hear the wolf packs howling, and knew that Nona and Justice had shape-shifted into their werewolf personas, and broken heartedly she cried very softly for those dear innocent children that had been cursed and had to live as outcasts for the rest of their lives.

She heard voices and the strange sounds that the camels made. The caravan was resting, but it would only be long enough to eat and give the camels time to drink their fill from the oasis that they had always stopped at. One of the young men came to see if she had woken up. Ella was terrified when she saw him kneel down next to her, and he was very aware of her fear. He tried to show her with hand movements and quieting gestures that she was in no danger, then he brought her some water, and told the leader that she was awake. He went at once to Ella and tried to communicate with her in the very limited English that he could speak." You not be fright ma'am, us will not hurt, take to home we stay, one week to walk" "Thank you very much, you are kind, I don't know how far I am from my own home"

The weather was very strange, you fried in the day, and froze at night, and many times they were delayed because of the unending sand storms, and the wind that almost cut you in half. It took longer than seven days to get to their home, but when they arrived all the people that lived in that area came to greet them. The leader explained how they had found Ella, and that is why they brought her home. Everybody understood only to well what can happen out in the desert after all that is where they lived. Ella was welcomed together with those that had just returned from the long journey. They prepared a feast, of roast meat on a spit, and some bread that was flat and cooked over the hot flames after the meat. They also drank a liquid that they called tea, it was very palatable, and Ella felt thankful for all that they did to make her welcome. She slept in a tent with the other young unmarried woman at night and shared in the daily duties.

Ella thanked the Great Spirit and the Angels every night for once again giving her a home, with wonderful people. She fitted in well and learned to speak their language, in a matter of three months. Ella missed mom and dad and her brothers, but she had no idea of how to find them again, and she never knew in which direction the caravan was going. With every full moon Ella cried herself to sleep praying for the victims of the cruel curse that they lived with. Ella was so used to having to be on the move from time to time, that she adapted very well to the Nomadic lifestyle. She also made friends with all the woman in the camp, and noticed that the men never came to the tent of the unmarried woman. She was grateful for that and thanked her little Angel and dear Prudence for keeping her safe. Life on the move had indeed become her way of living, ever since she was a child. However there were those wonderful cave days with her mommy Ester and the family where she had settled and stayed for a number of years, the happiest in her life. One night a man came to the camp on a camel, and asked if he could stay for a few days. The leader gave him permission and he slept in the tent with the unmarried men. The next morning when they were all gathered for tea and bread, he saw Ella for the first time. He went over to talk to her, and she saw that he had the same light brown skin and blue eyes that she had. It was love at first sight for both of them. They chatted all day and well into the night, and told their life history to each other.

His name was Paul and he told her that he was also an adopted son of her mom and dad, this he knew by the names of the twins and mom and dad's name. His mother had left him with them to go and look for his father, but never returned. No one knows what happened to her. Ella was so happy, as she had asked the Great Spirit and the Angels, "Please do not let this be another brother of mine, I love this man so much." Her prayer was answered as he was no relation to her at all" Then he said that he was going home to mom and dad and the twins.

"Do you want to come with me Ella?" "OH! Yes, yes, I do she said" Paul told the leader that Ella was going home with him and that they would leave in the early evening. A large food and water parcel was packed for the long way home, and they left just before sunset. They walked along for many hours and then Paul said that they must rest, and also the camel needed a drink. He put a covering of some sort on the sand, and got one of the food packs and a bottle of water out. They sat down and ate, dried meat and dates and drank some water. Then Paul packed what was left over back into the food parcel and they just looked at the stars, for a while. Ella told Paul that she was so sorry that she had not found the plant that would relieve mom's pain." Do not worry Ella I have some dried plants that the Nomads always use for pain, and I know that it will help her" She was so relieved that she clapped her hands in excitement, and thanked her Angels for sending this man.

Then Paul took Ella in his arms and kissed her tenderly, and that night Ella experienced the love of a good man for the first time ever.

The night passed to quickly for Ella and Paul, and the sunrise heralded the day and another long walk in the direction of home. They still had many miles to go, and Ella knew that there would be other nights like the last one, she only hoped that there would be the same ecstasy. She was hopelessly lost in the ardent love that she felt for Paul, and was sure that all the days and nights would be like this for the rest of their lives.

The heat was almost unbearable and Ella often thought that she would faint, but when Paul realized that the heat was taking its toll on Ester he stopped the camel and put a ground covering down in its shadow for Ella to lie down and rest for a while and also have a snack and a long drink of water. When she felt better they continued on their journey, after hours of walking she could see a mirage again in the heat waves ahead. Looming up in this Mirage she saw not one large rock but three and something else that she could not quite make out.

"Where are we now Paul and what are those things that I can see? or am I suffering from delusions. I do not remember coming this way before.?" "You came this way with the nomads that I found you with but you were unconscious my dear. We are in the Egyptian desert Ella and those things that you can see are the three pyramids and the other thing is known as the Sphinx the great God of the east. We are going to stop there for a few days so that you can explore them with me and we can also have a rest while we are there. We have a very long way still to go before we get home again. You see while you were with the Nomads you were on the move all the time and that is why you don't realize just how far from home you actually were my dearest little one.

Chapter 13

They reached a small settlement not far from the great stone structures, where they could rent a room for themselves and a stall for the camel. That night they went to bed after a light meal, and while saying their prayers Ella and Paul could hear wolves howling while the light of the moon shone into the room. Yes it was a full moon and their prayers were for the safety of Nona and Justice and all the victims of the dreaded lycanthrope curse. Paul held Ella in his arms and comforted her while her body trembled and the tears flowed freely down her cheeks. They were tears caused by the bitter memories that came flooding back every time that she heard the wolf packs howling. Ella was grateful that the Great Spirit God had replaced the abusive swine men that had abused her with a gentle, and compassionate man that loved and tenderly cared for her.

During the night they were awakened by the violent shaking of the earth, terrified people were screaming and running around trying to find their loved ones, as some of the rooms had collapsed and disappeared into large holes in the desert sand. Rumours were going around that the ancient Sphinx had sunk deeper into the continuously shifting sand. It had been foretold that when the great god of the east started to sink a considerable measure in relation to its size, into a cavity forming under its base, there would be catastrophes in Egypt that had never been heard of in any lifetime. Anubis the god of the underworld appeared and stood at attention in expectation of the appearance of the great god of the east known as the father of terror. His spirit had been cursed and he had been entombed in the stone body of the Sphinx while physically alive when it was being constructed by the ancient civilization on Atlantis, and then it was levitated and transported via the frequency of sound and placed in the desert directly under the constellation of Leo where it has stood ever since. The earthquake was so violent that the base of the Sphinx shattered and fell into the abyss that had formed right under it. There was a mighty wolf howl that was so loud that the acoustic sound of his voice reverberated all over the country announcing his freedom and liberation. Every wolf in the country joined in this great celebration and the full moon turned blood red. His reign of terror had now begun, and all those that had never revered him since their own incarnation started trembling in fear. They were all terrified at the thought of what he would do and how he would reign as a free spirit-god of the east. Anubis went forward to greet him and congratulate him on his escape from his stone prison, crouching down in submission although he was a God himself. This pleased the father of terror and he told Anubis that he was going to glide all through the cosmos as he had become bored in this place of his captivity of more than four thousand five hundred years However he was now going to give Anubis total control over the East in addition to his title as God of the underworld, and whatever law that he made must be obeyed or the perpetrator would be cursed and entombed in stone while still alive just as he had been all those years ago on Atlantis. Then he bid farewell to the new ruler and went off on his journey to explore the universe, not realizing that he was no longer a powerful ruler, but just an ordinary spirit that would be subject to the Great Spirit and all his commands.

Paul and Ella having witnessed all this knew that they would have to cower and submit to the great God Anubis using the tactics that he himself had displayed before the father of terror. The next day at sunrise Anubis announced that he would grant the wish of any person that was just visiting Egypt or passing through. This would be his gift in celebration of his new title as God of the east and the underworld. Paul said "Now is our chance Ella we must approach him very humbly and ask him to remove the Lycanthropic curse on all those that were born during the time of the full moon while the wolf packs gather and howl" "Yes Paul you are right let us go now before he changes his mind" When they were in the presence of the Great Anubis they fell on their knees and crawled on the ground before him keeping their heads down. When they were summoned they kept their pose and waited for him to speak. This impressed him very much and made him proud to honour his word. "Speak mortal beings and tell me what you want and I will grant your wishes" Paul spoke and told the great God all about the wishes that they begged him to grant and why. "Yes I will reverse all the curses of the Lycanthrope from your family here on earth and release all those souls that had the same curse and have been in the underworld since their physical death. I will do this in honour of the great god of terror who himself had received the identical curse when he was a being in Atlantis". Anubis the Jackal shape-shifted into a wolf and howled with supernatural vocal ability and by doing so he was announcing to the world that the curse had been removed for all time, from this family and their descendants as well as the souls of their departed ancestors. Paul and Ella graciously thanked him and when he dismissed them they kept their pose and crawled backwards away from him until well out of sight then they stood up and ran as fast as possible to get away from there.

The camel was nowhere to be found so they had to go all the way on foot. So they gathered all the edible dried fruit and meat that was available and took a few containers for water with them for the long journey, they were also blessed with a sand covering on which to lay when they rested, that a very compassionate person had given them. They travelled at night and took their direction from the position of the stars. Ella's little angel also told them when to veer off course for a while because there was an oasis nearby, and so although they had no idea how long the journey actually was they were able to remain sufficiently hydrated and strong enough to complete the distance home.

In other parts of the world as the full blood moon was declining amazing things were happening. Justice and Nona were on their way back to the cave while still in werewolf form as they had to leave the wolf packs before sunrise because they would shape-shift at the first light of dawn. When they got there they were surprised to see that Prudence had materialized and in her physical form as a woman she had been healed and complete. No more wounds were on her body and she had both her eyes and her feet. Justice and Nona were in awe and stood still not knowing what had happened. Prudence ran forward with outstretched arms and hugged them both needless to say they all cried and laughed at the same time, overcome with sheer joy. Then they went into the cave and Prudence told them how the Lycanthrope curse had been removed for all time. She told them that they could now go home to Ella and live as normal human beings for the first time in their lives. She promised to guide them to Ella and that she would always protect them from out of her new spirit world.

Justice and Nona decided that they would start on the long journey the following day and were in eager anticipation as to what reaction they would get from Ella. So they loaded up with food and plenty of water in the same way that Ella had when they all left the cave due to the long drought. They were guided and protected by the little angel and Prudence all the way. It was a long and hazardous journey and they were often to tired to move on, so they rested for a day and then went on again as they were slowly but surely running out of food and water, taking a longer rest could lead to starvation and dehydration, so they pushed on and on, it seemed like the journey would never end.

Chapter 14

Ella saw the huge rock looming up in the distance and recognizing it knew that Paul would stop there for something to eat and drink, and rest in its most welcome shade. The sun was blazing hot so much so that mirages appeared in every direction. When they reached the rock Paul put a covering over the sand and they had the usual dried meat and dates that had been given to them by other nomads going in the opposite direction and thankfully a drink of water. They were both exhausted, so Paul took Ella in his arms and they went to sleep.

When Paul woke up the sun was setting, so he woke Ella and folding the covering that had served as their bed wrapped it over the food pack and water canister for sustenance along the way. Having done this they set off for the final miles of their journey during the cool night hours. As the time passed slowly they began to sing songs, and tell jokes to amuse themselves. Although they were going at the usual pace the time seemed to go faster, and soon the corona of the sun appeared, beaconing the journey's end. Within the hour the outline of the house was visible. Ella and Paul thanked the Holy Spirit and the Angels, for a safe journey.

Jared was weeding in the vegetable patch when they arrived. They both called out to him and Ella went running with outstretched arms and tears of joy, as she kept repeating "daddy, daddy." Jared got up with much difficulty and was almost knocked over when Ella flung herself into his arms. Then Paul got there and also hugged Jared. He was speechless and just cried and hugged them for a long time, Ella asked him "where is mom?" "Mom is in bed, she can hardly move on her own anymore, and I have to do most things for her'. I am so glad that you are home Ella, what happened to you?. Let us first go to your mom and then you and Paul can tell us what happened". Menlo could not believe her eyes when she saw them both. The welcome they got was a repeat of the one they just had from dad, but with many more gestures.

After they had all settled down Paul helped mom to the table and Ella made coffee, with bread and jam for a snack. Paul related the whole story of how Ella went missing and how she was found, also how he had met up with her, and the discovery that they had the same adoptive parents. He told them about the journey home and how they had fallen in love. The old people were delighted and insisted that they have a wedding when the twins get home in a week's time. The next day Paul went into town and bought a wedding dress for Ella, and some snacks for the table. When he got home Ella was baking a fruit cake, using a recipe that mom had. It had been in her family since she could remember. Paul helped Ella to clean and tidy up, in preparation for the twin's home coming tomorrow. Ella tried on the wedding dress, and it was a perfect fit, but mom insisted that Paul could not see her in it until her twin brothers walked her down the aisle in the beautiful garden.

The next day was beautiful, not to hot or cold, and while having breakfast the twins opened the door and came in shouting "We are home, we are home" then they kept quiet and just stared at the sight that met their eyes. Now the whole family was reunited and there was great excitement when all the stories were told. But there was a great deal of sadness and Menlo and family cried soulful tears when Ella finally told the family about the Lycanthrope curse and how she had to leave Nona and Justice to fend for themselves, and that they had to give dear Prudence a burial at sea so that no starving stray animal would dig her up and devour her crippled body. Hardly had the words been spoken when they all heard voices shouting "Hello, Hello is there anyone home?" Ella recognizing the voices but hardly daring to believe her ears, jumped up and ran to open the door. When she saw Nona and Justice standing there she opened her arms and hugged them both and with tears in her eyes she fainted without uttering a word.

Both her brothers ran to assist her and help her gain consciousness, while Paul went to talk to the people that had caused his beloved Ella to faint. There was no doubt in his mind as to who they were, because Nona was the splitting image of Ella. He introduced himself and then welcomed them to come inside and meet their family.

Menlo and Jared hugged them and told them that they were their grandparents and everyone was overwhelmed. A delicious meal was prepared by Ella for them and while sitting at the table she noticed that the tip of Nona's ear had been torn and asked her how it had happened. She told them all and said that it had healed in a lump because the torn piece was not completely torn off by the werewolf that was opposing her for rank in the pack, but it was very sore and had taken ages to heal. Tom and Matt both examined the wound and said that they could operate on it and make it look much better if she was willing to undergo such an operation. Then they explained the procedure to her and she said that she would be very grateful if they would do it. The next day they got their instruments out of their medical bags and the operation was done on granny Menlo's kitchen table that had been scrubbed cleaner than ever before. It was a great success and was completely healed in two weeks with much praise and thanks to Tom and Matt and the Great Spirit god and the Angels.

Justice asked Ella for Nona's hand in marriage and she gladly gave her consent. Then Paul suggested that they make it a double wedding while the family were all together and before the brothers had to go back to their jobs as ships doctors. Everyone cheered and the preparations started that very day. Paul took Justice back to the shop where he had purchased Ella's wedding dress and they bought one for Nona. The date had been set so they only had a few days in which to do all the necessary things.

Chapter 15

Everyone got up early on the chosen morning as this was the happiest occasion for this family. Today was Ella and Paul's wedding day. Mom and Dad got dressed in their best clothes, and so did the twins. Paul and Justice bought grey suits for this occasion and they looked like princes. Mom sat on a chair in the shade of the "wedding tree" and Dad stood next to her, ready to perform the service. Paul and Justice stood next to Dad waiting for Ella and Nona to arrive. The twins were on either side of them each holding an arm, and announced the arrival of the brides by both singing "HERE COME THE BRIDES" Ella and Nona were beautiful and so were their dresses. Paul and Justice said that there could never ever have been more beautiful brides in all history. Then each couple linked arms and took turns to stand before dad and mom, and dad did the service. When he asked "WHO GIVES THIS WOMAN TO THIS MAN?" The twins got up and said we do. The service concluded and every one congratulated the newlyweds, and then the party started and went on until dawn.

Paul and Ella decided to spend their wedding night under the stars in dad's olive orchard, and "Oh! What a night it was, it really was, a night to remember for a lifetime" and Justice and Nona decided to spend their night in the dunes not far from the house. It was full moon and just a single howl was heard. Justice and Nona were so grateful to the Great Spirit God and the angels that Ella had taught them about, when they remained in the human form for the first time. They got up early and went into the house for breakfast. Dad and the twins were sitting leaning on their arms with their heads resting on them, and Paul said "Yes, yes, yes, they must have a terrible hangover Ella!!" Then Dad shook his head and said "No not a hangover, Mom passed away during the night, the twins have examined her and, came to the conclusion that she had a heart attack" This was bad news and both Paul and Ella ran into her room, and kissed her and said prayers for her, Ella knew not to question but to accept that mom's season of life was over and her time had come to return to the Great Spirit Source. When Justice and Nona arrived Paul told them that granny Menlo had crossed over into the spirit realm during the night. They were broken hearted but also grateful that they had known her even if it was for such a short time.

Sadly and with many tears her four boys dug a grave under the wedding tree, as that had been her favourite spot to sit and rest. Ella prepared her body for burial, while dad just sat and stared into the endless sky.

When everything was ready they carried mom's body out and laid it in the grave. Then covered it over with the earth, and surrounded it with stones. Then Ella prayed using the same words that she had used when she buried her beloved mommy so long ago. The weeks passed and the daily routine went on calmly and quietly until the twins had to go back to their ships again.

When they left Dad hugged them both and gave them his blessing, saying "I think this will be my last goodbye to you both, as I do not think that I will see you again" They both assured him that he would be here and that they would see him again. With waves and some tears they set off back to the sea. Paul and Ella, Justice and Nona were very happy and looked after dad as best they could. Time went by and Dad saw the twins for another three visits, and then he got a very "bad flu." That is how they described it as they never knew any medical terms. Dad was ill for a short while and then he went to join mom for eternity. Paul, Ella, Justice and Nona laid him to rest in a grave they dug next to moms. They decided to stay on the plot and live the rest of their lives there, at the only home they had shared. One bright morning Nona and Justice came to the breakfast table and Justice announced that Nona was pregnant and that the baby would be born during the Twin's next vacation. Time seemed to fly because work on the plot occupied most of the men's time, and the two women were kept busy cleaning and cooking and making clothes for the baby that was soon to be born.

At last the long awaited call "Hello, hello is anyone there" was heard by all and the family rushed out to meet and welcome the twin Dr's. They were overjoyed that Nona was pregnant and that they would be there to deliver her baby when the time came. It was well into the second week of their vacation when Nona went to Ella during the night and told her that she had very bad pain. Paul went and woke Tom and Matt and told them that Nona's time had come. They put a blanket on the already scrubbed and disinfected kitchen table and told Nona to get on to it. Then they said that Justice could attend the birth if he wanted to but asked Paul to take Ella for a walk and that they would call when he could bring her back again.

Paul took Ella into the Olive grove and they walked up and down the rows of trees to pass the time. Paul sang lively happy songs to Ella to try and distract her from what was going on at home. Suddenly Ella stopped walking and froze while looking up at the sky. Paul followed her stone like gaze and saw that it was full moon. Taking her in his arms he reminded her that the curse had been removed but she trembled and silent tears ran down her cheeks while she rested her head on Paul's shoulder. They stood and hugged each other for what seemed like an eternity, and with great relief they heard no wolf howl and no pack gathering howls.

At that moment the twins called out saying "You can come back now granny and grandpa it is all over" Paul and Ella ran to the house and were presented with a baby each by the proud father. No words can describe the emotions that the family experienced, two perfect beautiful babies had been born. One boy and one girl, Ella went over to Nona and hugged and kissed her own precious daughter, congratulations were given by all. Then there was a knock at the door but when they opened it there was no one there, however when looking down there were two unexpected gifts on the step. Paul picked them up and took them in to

Nona, who opened them up in the presence of all. When the contents were revealed Ella burst into tears and as usual when she was overwhelmed she fainted. Tom went to help her over the emotion that had brought this fainting spell on, and when she recovered she said "Two goat hides and two rabbit furs this is from my Mommy Ester who helped me to give birth to my babies, and she used skins just like these to keep us warm, thank you mommy Ester for being here to see your great grandchildren and for the most treasured gift in the world."

The twins had to leave a week after the babies were born and so they organized a baptism under the tree that held so many memories. Then they had a very jolly party that continued well into the early morning hours as all the parties had done because there were so few reasons for a celebration. Justice and Nona decided to name the babies after their great grandparents Menlo and Jared. Every year they welcomed the twins for their holidays, in this haven that mom and dad had given them, their very own garden paradise.

They always had family prayers of thanks to the Great Spirit and the Angels for the wonderful parents that they had, and for this home and the miracles that they had received all the years of their lives, and that Ella was not a fugitive anymore, and Justice, Nona, and the babies were free to live as normal human beings until their season came to cross over to the realm of spirit.

THE END